PANDORA'S GUN

Fairwood Press books
by James Van Pelt

Flying in the Heart of the Lafayette Escadrille
The Radio Magician
Summer of the Apocalypse
The Last of the O-Forms
Strangers and Beggars

Advance Praise for James Van Pelt's
Pandora's Gun

"*Pandora's Gun* is a tender look at two teenagers who must save the world from a most dangerous thing. Van Pelt teaches high school, and his experience clearly helps him create heartbreakingly realistic teens for protagonists in a classic SF adventure story. *Pandora's Gun* comes complete with a childhood friendship that's falling apart, old relationships becoming new again, and families under threat. It's also incredibly well-written. Van Pelt is, as he always is, brilliant."   —Brenda Cooper, author of *Edge of Dark*

"Van Pelt, one of the finest short story writers of our time, has written a YA novel. *Pandora's Gun* has a kind of sweet old timey feel to it. . . I really did enjoy this short novel that asks a lot of wonderful "what if" questions in the traditions of classic science fiction."   —*Genrefluence*

"An ingenious thriller set in a backdrop of current events like hackers vs. firewalls, cell phones vs. jamming, blanket school emails, phone encryption vs. GPS—all filtered through characters who manage to stay one step ahead of their pursuers via loyalty, friendship, shared memories of childhood, and parents who don't have a clue but love their teens. To those who know James Van Pelt, the educator, there is almost an Easter Egg quality to his protagonist's "super power"—being good at writing papers for school. These papers and their subjects are how VanPelt packs layers of meaning into a story you could wholeheartedly recommend to your favorite teen or tween, and enjoy on a deeper level as an adult."   —*Abyss & Apex*

"Van Pelt is a high school teacher, and his familiarity with teenagers and the teenage condition shines through in this story. There's something for everyone here, from the teen who will recognize aspects of him or herself in the characters, to the adult who will experience a wistful nostalgia for younger—but not necessarily simpler—times."   —*SFReader.com*

"A young-adult thriller about teens who discover an advanced weapon with plenty of catastrophic applications, and must flee the two different groups searching their town for it. . . . The strength of the novel lies in the viewpoint character, Peter Van Meek, a decent kid for whom this is just one of the issues he has to figure out, among them who he wants to be. A really sweet developing friendship between him and the girl next door, too.
—Adam-Troy Castro, author of *Emissaries from the Dead*

PANDORA'S
GUN

JAMES
VAN PELT

FAIRWOOD PRESS
Bonney Lake, WA

PANDORA'S GUN
A Fairwood Press Book
August 2015
Copyright © 2015 by James Van Pelt

Fairwood Press
21528 104th Street Court East
Bonney Lake, WA 98391
www.fairwoodpress.com

Front cover image by
Kuldar Leement
Book design by
Patrick Swenson

ISBN13: 978-1-933846-53-8
First Fairwood Press Edition: August 2015
Printed in the United States of America

To every student who loves to read.
I saw you with that book in class, reading quietly,
rebelliously, on your own. You are a special tribe. My tribe.

1

Much later, Peter remembered a lesson from last year's 9th grade mythology class. They had just finished learning about Pandora and how her curiosity released the world's woes. Someone said, "That's sort of like Eve in the garden of Eden. If she hadn't messed around, eating that apple, we'd still be in paradise." Somebody else said, "And Helen is the reason Troy was destroyed and so many heroes died." The first boy laughed. "So, women caused humanity's problems."

Mrs. Stiles looked at the class for a minute before saying, "All that you can conclude from so many stories about women bringing trouble into the world is that the myths were written by men."

But Peter Van Meer wasn't thinking about mythology when he was at the dump, wearing yellow dishwashing gloves while searching for treasure, or if he was, it was about thrown away lamps that hold genies and three wishes. At the beginning of the summer, he'd reached under a long, sun-burnished metal plank, and plunged his hand into a rotting mess of sun-warmed meat swimming with maggots, and even days later he thought he could smell it on his fingers, so he'd taken the gloves from the kitchen to scavenge.

Today, though, in the September heat, he didn't whiff anything sketchy, and the rustling leaves from the elms and willows surrounding the clearing seemed particularly bright and cheery.

He wasn't worried about the gross out.

Over the last hour, he'd scooted down from the lip of the depression that held the dump, working his way through the leavings. The trash pit was only thirty feet across. He could sort through the mess in a couple of hours. Most of the trash seemed to be metal, although he'd examined with interest a broken doll made of a very light wood, and what might have been a book, except the pages were too long and blank. He'd also found and discarded dozens of silvery beer cans, except that they didn't have labels, and whatever they had held didn't smell like beer.

His best friend, Dante Blevins, maintained that the dump was a secret government waste site. "That's why the trash keeps changing," he said the last time they'd gone treasure hunting. "They put their classified stuff here *temporarily*, and then recycle it elsewhere."

Peter sat back and rested his weight on his hands behind him. He hadn't pointed out to Dante that there wasn't a road to the clearing, nor any evidence that anyone visited the site. The winding, nearly invisible trail they followed to get here never had other footprints. The only way the dump was a government site would be if the trash was airlifted in and out, and the clearing wasn't *that* far out of town that people wouldn't notice a low-flying copter.

Still, the contents of the dump did change. Someone put new trash in and pulled old trash out.

He leaned forward to move another metal sheet. This one was four feet long and a couple of feet wide, but thin as a road sign. Like most of the stuff in the dump, it had no writing. Almost everything he found lacked identifying information. He wondered if he should take a picture to post to his on-line friends. Maybe they would know what the trash was. No, then he might have to explain why he wanted to know and where he'd found it. Having Dante know about the dump was bad enough. Dante didn't have Peter's sense of wonder. Peter thought of himself as having scientific curiosity. You could tell a lot by what people threw out, he thought. Digging in a dump was modern archeology.

Dante, though, wanted to try to sell the metal as scrap, as if anyone would want to backpack out heavy hunks of busted machinery. The materials had no serial numbers. No labels or stamps. Nothing that identified where the scraps came from or their function. Occasionally, he longed for the familiar: a dented soup can, maybe, or a greasy pizza box. Mostly broken things filled the dump. Discarded things. Gears, levers, hinges, boxes that wouldn't open, springs, thick bottles that looked more like crystal than glass (most were chipped or cracked), lengths of corroded wire, worn cloth that wouldn't tear, wheels like car wheels but too narrow and made from a stiff leather instead of rubber. And occasionally, smelly things. He looked at his yellow gloves ruefully.

And sometimes, there were treasures.

He kept the best ones on a shelf in his room. His favorite was a small statue of a bare-chested man, about the size of a little kid's soccer trophy. When he'd found it, the figure had been reaching up with both hands as if in supplication. The metal was copper-colored and soft. He could dent it with his fingernail, but the dent filled within a half hour, and the statue was unmarked again. The statue moved, too. In the months it had sat on his shelf, it had gone from the hands in the air pose, to semi-kneeling, hands down, head turned to the side, as if it thought something approached from behind. The change was so slow that Peter had taken measurements to compare from week to week. It gradually, but definitely changed position.

He'd found a broken sword in the pile another time, made of a metal that always felt cooler than it should. A hard leather or plastic binding protected the hilt, and the inch-wide blade had been snapped off, leaving only a couple of inches of an unbelievably sharp edge. He'd lost skin off the end of his finger testing it.

The metal sheet resisted efforts to move it. He tugged, putting his back into it, and was rewarded with a budge. On the third attempt, the sheet snapped free and flew several feet away, landing with a clang. A panicked rabbit scurried out from under the jumbled pile on the dump's other edge, and didn't even look back as it dashed into the forest. Peter's laugh stopped in his throat when he saw what he'd uncovered: a black duffle bag, closed tight.

He lifted it by the handle, surprised by the weight. It wasn't zipped—nothing he'd found in the dump ever had anything about it that seemed familiar, even something as mundane as a zipper. The bag opened along a long seam, but the edges separated more as if theys were magnetic or attached with an exceptionally fine Velcro, parting smoothly and quietly. Peter stared into the bag, trying to decide what he was looking at.

Translucent bricks, maybe four inches by three inches, lined the bag's bottom. Sunlight fell into the bag, but the bricks absorbed the light without reflection. On top of the bricks rested an odd instrument, like just the grip half of a pistol. Where he'd expect to find a barrel, the pistol flared into a fist-sized lump. It felt heavy and solid in his hand, a dull gray with a purple sheen in the bright sun.

He set it aside. The little bricks seemed more interesting. He picked one up; it felt for a second like it buzzed. He wondered if it was electrical. When he held it up to the sun, an incredibly fine wire grid inside reflected a constellation of glitters. The brick itself looked like Plexiglas, but it was way too heavy to be plastic. He turned the brick over. He guessed there might be a couple hundred in the duffle bag.

A bird screeched in a tree by the clearing, and then beat its wings hard as it took off. Peter glanced around. The sun had moved several degrees across the sky. His phone showed him that it was almost an hour later than he thought it was. He looked at the bag thoughtfully. Had he lost time while looking into it? There was something hypnotic about the bricks. He couldn't tell in the afternoon sun, but he suspected they might glow in the dark. There was a depth to their translucence.

Later, he thought about Pandora opening the box. At least she'd been warned to keep the box closed. Considering what happened, Peter thought that a warning would have been fair.

Reluctantly, he returned the brick he held back into the gap he'd created by pulling it out.

The truncated pistol didn't fit his grip well. Whoever held it had bigger hands than he did. Careful to keep his finger off the unguarded trigger, he examined it from all sides. Grooves crossed the handle. The trigger curved out, a small sliver just big enough to wrap his finger around. The lump that constituted the rest of the instrument had a misshapen, almost handmade look. There was no hole where he'd expect to see one if it was a pistol, but clearly it was designed to be held and pointed.

Feeling a little silly, he aimed it at the nearest tree, a fifty-foot tall elm whose leaves would turn a brilliant yellow in a few weeks, after the first frost. He pulled the trigger.

A screen popped into view above his hand, ten inches by eight inches, about the size of a piece of typing paper. Startled, Peter released the trigger. The screen vanished.

What he should have done, Peter thought, was to put the weird looking instrument back into his bag. His mother had told him when he was little that if he found something, it wasn't lost. "It belongs to somebody," she'd said. The bag belonged to someone. The bricks and the strange gun were not his to play with, but he didn't think that at the time.

He looked into the woods. No one could possibly see him here. He was alone. Tentatively, he pulled the trigger again. The screen was a projection of some kind, a hologram, but when he touched it, there was resistance. It displayed a series of icons, like a phone. None of the shapes were familiar. He pressed one, and the grip clicked. Something mechanical happened inside and the icons disappeared on the screen, replaced by a crosshair.

He pointed at the same tree, pulled the trigger, and flames flew from it from root to highest twig in a deep roar. Smoke and steam rose into the sky. Birds took wing from nearby trees, heading away from the huge torch.

For a moment, Peter stood frozen, finger still compressing the trigger, blinking against the sudden brightness.

Carefully, he put the gun back in the bag and closed it. The tree's flames warmed his face, even in the sun's heat, and smelled of boiling sap and crisping leaves. A thick branch mid-way up, hissed as if steam were escaping, and then exploded, bringing down a third of the upper branches, popping and crackling in a startlingly loud rush.

Thank goodness it's been a rainy end of the summer, thought Peter, too stunned to think anything else. Burning limbs quickly flared out in the damp bushes and grass that made up the underbrush, and within a few minutes, the flames flickered out, leaving a sad, smoky and steaming ruin. A few burnt leaves, turned black and limp, clung to the now bare branches.

He took out his phone and texted Dante: "Meet me. 6:00. Important."

If Pandora had a phone, would she have texted her friends? OMG! YOU WON'T BELIEVE WHAT JUST HAPPENED.

2

Peter and Dante started preschool together, and they'd been best friends since. They learned to ride a bike on the same day. They built tree houses and buried forts. Any book Peter read, he leant to Dante, and Dante did the same, although Peter leaned toward history and biographies, while Dante mostly read horror and true crime.

They'd walked to school together for ten years. Peter would sling his backpack over his shoulder, cross the street, and then walk two blocks to get to Dante's house. He'd stand on the sidewalk until Dante bounded out, grinning, ready to tell a joke. Peter remembered the day that Dante had looked at him, full of concern. It might have been when they were in second grade. "Your epidermis is showing," he'd said. Peter glanced down at his zipper, embarrassed, which set Dante to laughing. "Epidermis is your skin, you goof. Everyone's epidermis is showing."

They trick-or-treated together in the fall, and signed up for the same swimming lessons in the spring. They joined T-ball on the same team and played long games of one-on-one basketball on Peter's driveway.

Both were tall for their age and slender. Dante's blond hair framed a face that smiled often, and dark eyes that laughed seldom. Peter kept his red hair short, and was the more serious of the two, although Dante could make him laugh.

They synced their first smart phones when they were twelve

so they'd know where the other was. A month into 6ᵗʰ grade, Peter caught bronchitis and missed two weeks of school. He'd taken comfort in watching the dot on the map that represented Dante's position. Peter could see when he switched classes. He saw when he went to lunch, and he knew when Dante was walking toward his house to bring him homework and share the day's news.

Until last year, they talked about the same movies, complained about the same classes, liked long, philosophical discussions about the same topics. Peter was the better student, while Dante was more athletic, although he didn't play sports for the high school.

Lately, though, Peter found himself looking at this best friend with surprise. Dante argued more. He wanted to go places that didn't interest Peter. He hung out with kids Peter didn't know. Sometimes Peter wondered what happened. Maybe an alien replaced him with an exact duplicate. Did I hurt his feelings? There were times when he felt like they were on slick ice, sliding apart.

Two months earlier, Peter had waited on the sidewalk in front of Dante's house for ten minutes before he went to the door and knocked. Dante opened the door, wearing an old T-shirt and sweatpants. His eyes were bloodshot. "Not going to school today," he'd said. "A little too much of Dad's Johnny Walker last night." Dante started drinking on the sly months ago, but he hadn't confronted Peter with the evidence so clearly before. Peter turned the significance of that news over and over as he walked the rest of the way to school. He remembered when they'd agreed a couple of years past that they would never do something stupid, like drink or smoke or do drugs.

A year ago, Peter would have shared his discoveries with Dante without a thought. They moved like a pair of birds linked with a silver strand, but a year is a long time when you have just entered your teens. In a year, Dante faded a little, became fuzzy in Peter's mind, and when Peter looked at him, he didn't quite see his own reflection. They hadn't walked to school together since that morning.

So Peter carried the heavy duffle bag home, hid it under his bed, and put the gun in a backpack to meet Dante.

3

The day before, Peter spent the afternoon with Student Senate, cleaning out an abandoned house near the school. They had to log 100 community service hours in the year, and this was the project they'd chosen for November. The house represented the last remnant of a subdivision that went up when the coal mine opened on BLM land nearby, and was abandoned when the mine went out of business after a few years. The cheaply-made houses had no resale value, so over time the city had been razing them to keep the drug dealers out. Now the property was lined by streets and sidewalks, but the lots were scraped clean except for this last house.

Peter liked abandoned houses, just as he liked landfills and the secret dump in the woods. Treasure is everywhere! he thought. Standing in a back bedroom, he filled a trash bag with water-soaked *National Geographics*. A girl complained from another room that the house smelled funky, and she worried about spiders. Peter smiled. He liked the community service hours for Senate. In a couple of weeks, they'd be raking leaves from old folks' yards, and after that they would spring into action with shovels and buckets of road salt anytime it snowed.

Sometimes the old people would give them tips, but they lived on fixed income, so it might be a plate of cookies, or once, memorably, three delicious lemon meringue pies.

But as much as helping out felt good, he liked digging

through refuse. It's an odd hobby, he thought as he picked up a moldy shoe from behind the magazines. He looked at it critically. At one time, it had been a brown businessman's shoe. Now, the toe had separated from the sole, and the sole itself had a hole in the bottom. He'd heard somewhere that bums would line the bottoms of their holed shoes with newspaper to protect their feet. How many miles had this shoe seen? What was the person like who'd bought it? Did the man picture that one day a high school kid would be holding this same shoe, wondering about him? Had he lived in this room? Did he have big dreams about the money he'd make from mining? Maybe he'd been a foreman. This wasn't a worker's shoe. Or maybe this was his Sunday go-to-church shoe. A shoe like this could tell a hundred stories.

That's what he liked about the dump in the woods. Every scrap hinted at some story. Everything broken once worked and was vital. An abandoned house had once been new and filled with dreams. When he dug through the dump, he uncovered histories. This old house held echoes of the people who used to live here. Peter shivered in delight while looking at a closet filled with boxes waiting to be cleaned out.

He brought the shoe into a beam of light coming through a dusty window. Where he would have put his foot, if he were going to put the shoe on, a film of spider web covered the opening. Hanging to the underside, bouncing a little as Peter moved the shoe, clung a black widow, its red hourglass vividly visible.

Good thing I'm not arachnophobic, he thought as he put the shoe in the trash bag, along with the magazines.

He went to warn the rest of the class to be careful what they picked up.

4

At 6:00, the clear skies had given way to a storm front coming in from the west. The sun hid behind the dark clouds, and lightning flicked in their depths. The air had taken a damp, autumn feel, like winter emerging. Peter wished he'd brought a jacket. He and Dante cut through the high school's practice fields to the break in the split rail fence that separated the fields from the woods behind. On the school side of the fence, neatly lined soccer fields and mowed grass had a military order. On the other side, the wildwood defied pattern. Elms, willows, low, scraggly brush, haphazard weeds, and rotted leaves still piled from last winter, created an untamed woods. Their trail to the dump started there, although it wasn't much of a trail. Spiky brambles tugged at their sleeves as they pushed through.

Dante told a dirty joke that embarrassed Peter, who laughed, even though he didn't like jokes like that. Dante had been telling more of them lately and saying things like, "Check the rack on that girl." Peter purposefully wouldn't look, although sometimes he'd see what Dante was talking about before he could glance away. Dante snuck beers out of his stepdad's refrigerator, and offered to share with Peter. Dante had started smoking a month ago. But it wasn't just the change of habits. They'd sworn to each other that they would never do those things—Peter wished to remind Dante of that, but he couldn't bring himself to say it out loud.

Maybe all could be forgiven, but they didn't talk like they used to either. Conversations that would never stop now dwindled to uncomfortable pauses. Who do you talk to when you don't know how to talk to your best friend?

"We've never found anything that worked," said Dante. "Busted stuff, sure, but not a machine."

They'd walked about half the distance to the dump. In another quarter mile, they'd be there. The sky darkened even more, and a sudden rain pelted them. They took shelter under an elm, waiting for the squall to pass.

"Let me see," said Dante.

Rain pattered around them, but the thick canopy worked as an umbrella.

"Let's get to the burnt tree first." Peter felt the gun's weight in his pack and a reluctance now to show it.

"Did you find anything else? Anything we could sell?"

"I stopped looking after the tree blew up."

"I thought you said it burned."

Peter shrugged. "Whatever. The rain's stopped. Let's go."

Dante whistled when he saw the tree. Steam hissed out of a deep crack where water seeped in. The bark still felt warm. "You weren't kidding! That's awesome."

Peter put the backpack on the ground, opened it, and handed the gun to Dante.

"So, I pull the trigger to turn it on?" he said.

Peter pushed the gun away from him. "And be careful where you point it when you do."

The screen flared into view. Peter moved behind Dante so he could look over his shoulder. "That upside down Y with the apostrophes on either side was the one I pressed."

Dante ran his finger across the screen. The twelve icons vanished and were replaced by twelve new ones.

"It looks like Chinese," said Dante. He replaced the set of icons twice more before they saw the first set of symbols again.

"Wow, forty-eight choices. Do you think any of them are Netflix?"

Shadows dominated under the trees, and where the day had been cheery earlier, Peter felt nervous, like they should be hiding, like someone must be watching them. The duffle bag filled with oddly heavy bricks and this . . . whatever it was . . . made him think about those movies where some poor schmuck ended up with a Mafioso's drug money. The gun . . . tool . . . device could be many things, but it clearly wasn't his. Just like his mother had said, it belonged to somebody.

Dante touched an icon. The gun clicked as the screen vanished. "Here goes," Dante said as he held the gun at arm's length, pointing it at the already burned tree.

Peter wanted to cover his ears.

"Damn," said Dante, a tinge of surprise in his voice. "The forest is gone."

The trees stood as they did before, water dripping off the leaves. Overhead, thunder rumbled.

"It looks there to me."

"No, on the screen, the trees aren't there."

The screen had reappeared. Peter looked over Dante's shoulder. It showed a bare landscape. No trees or grass or brush. Just dirt and rock. Dante swung the gun from one view to the next. On the screen, all plants were gone.

A brown blob in an upper corner caught Peter's eye. "Go back. What's that?"

Dante squinted at the screen. "I think it's a squirrel." He moved his finger toward the screen, as if to touch it. "Oh, wow." When his finger grew close, the image magnified. It was a squirrel, one of about a dozen within view, all floating, it seemed, without support. They also found birds and a snake. Peter didn't know that snakes could be in the trees.

He looked away from the screen again. The forest stood unchanged, but now he knew the animals were hidden in the branches.

Dante turned so the gun was pointed at Peter. He laughed, hard. "You're naked, bud. Whew, you really should get a tattoo."

"Let me see that." The gun erased clothes! "The TSA would like this, I'd bet." Peter swung the gun up so he could only see Dante from the waist up. He moved his finger toward the screen to see how much it would magnify. Instead of growing larger, though, Dante's skin turned red in the screen, revealing meat and pulsing veins. "Whoa! I might not have any clothes, but you don't have any skin." When his finger got close enough, the image of Dante's face in the screen peeled away so that he became a sculpture of muscles and tendons. A little closer, and the bone surfaced through the fading flesh—an animated skull that stared back at him—and closer yet revealed the throbbing wet mass of Dante's brain.

Dante wasn't looking at him now, though. He bent to study the trail. "Somebody else has been here."

Peter released the trigger, turning the gun off. In the mud between Dante's feet glistened the footprint of a smooth-soled shoe. "That's got to be recent."

Lightning cracked hard, and the clouds opened, soaking them. Dante surveyed the forest in the rain and the cloud-caused dark, now almost impenetrable. "That's a recent print. Whoever made that could still be around."

The woods were no match for the downpour, and there was no safe place to shelter. They ran through the trees to the high school before splitting up for their homes.

5

After dinner, after Dad finally quit asking him about how his school day went and how his studies were going, and after Dad finally retired to his bedroom for the night, Peter could inspect the gun once again. He rubbed a towel over the backpack, carefully mopping up the moisture before removing the gun.

Outside, the storm had settled into a steady drizzle. Occasionally thunder grumbled in the distance.

The icon Dante had pressed looked like an open box, upside down over a squiggle. Peter activated it, then grunted in surprise. In the screen, the furniture, house and all the vegetation vanished. It was if he was sitting in a warm, dry bubble during a rain storm. Light from within the house showed water sheeting off the roof to the invisible gutters. The streetlights were gone, but their globes of light still hung above the street like Earthbound suns.

Peter swung the gun around. A cat on the other side of his bedroom wall sidled along the house, keeping out of the rain. Two birds, nestled side by side, hung suspended in the air where the big Maple that grew by his house stood. He panned the gun to reveal more. Twenty feet away, his father sat in his chair in his bedroom, reading. But there was no chair and no bedroom no book, and his Dad on the screen wasn't wearing clothes. The gun seemed to remove everything that wasn't landscape or living creature from the view. Who would need an app that did that?

Peter upped the magnification and saw into Christy Sanders' house, his next door neighbor. Her parents floated in what must have been their living room, bathed by a television's bluish and inconstant light. He didn't magnify them. There are some things the human eye is not intended to see, he thought. He was pretty sure that a pair of naked fifty-year-olds would burn his eyeballs out.

Christy herself lay on her bed, back to him. She'd sung the lead in the spring musical last year as a freshman. She was the sophomore pom-pom team captain, and a shoo-in for to be a part of Homecoming royalty in a couple weeks. She was also the only girl in school who Peter could talk to confidently. After all, she was just the neighbor girl. He'd watched her wrestling the trash cans to the alley on trash day, and he'd seen her changing the oil in her car (not very successfully, if the amount of oil on her shirt was an indication). They'd known each other for as long as Peter had known Dante, but sometime after they turned ten, they quit hanging out. She made other friends, and Peter and Dante became inseparable.

Peter didn't think of the implications of magnifying her image in time. She too was naked, partly silhouetted by her reading light that shone through her hair like a golden nimbus, and for a moment the way her bare hip curved into the small of her back stunned him.

He poked his finger at the screen twice to turn the gun off.

Later, after rehiding the duffle bag and gun in the back of his closet, under layers of old clothes and toys and school projects, he tried to sleep, but in the dark he kept seeing Christy on her bed. I'm not a creeper, he thought. I didn't spy on her on purpose. Still, when he closed his eyes, he saw how she rested her bare foot on her calf, how her leg bent gracefully, how in the invisible house on the invisible bed, covered with an invisible blanket, she'd looked like a mythical figure floating. Something out of Greek mythology. She belonged in Olympus.

I'm objectifying! he thought. I'm not thinking about her as a person!

When he fell asleep, though, after what seemed like hours, he didn't dream of Christy. What he dreamed instead were of footprints in the mud, and hosts of angry men searching for the bag in his closet. In the dream, they circled his house, then closed in. Nothing is truly lost, he thought. Everything belongs to somebody.

He woke before dawn and couldn't fall back to sleep. After a while, he unburied the duffle bag and took the gun out again, looked in the direction of Christy's house, but he didn't turn it on. He thought about it though.

As the sun rose, Peter slipped through the back door, duffle bag in hand, and put the gun in the trunk of the 1958 Ford Fairlane Dad had been restoring for the last half-dozen years. He couldn't think of a safer place to hide it.

6

Last year, when Peter was a freshman, the school newspa-per did an article on first kisses. Peter read the article with interest later. Most of the girls didn't think much of their first kisses, evidently. They said that either the kiss surprised them (one quote read, "Out of the blue! I reached for popcorn, and bam! Out of the blue!"), that the boy who kissed them was totally not who they wanted to be kissing, or that the kiss itself was sloppy, slurpy, or clumsy. One girl said he chipped her tooth. Another, somehow, got poked in the eye, and spent the rest of the evening being able to see clearly on only one side.

The boys told different stories. The girls, they said, thought they were great kissers, and their first kisses were "hot," "romantic," or both. One boy claimed he'd had so many first kisses that they blended together.

A student reporter, a girl with gold, wire-rimmed glasses, a splash of acne on her cheek, and a devastatingly nice smile, had interviewed Peter for the article. She gave him a short survey that included how old he was for his first kiss (Peter wrote, "13"), how romantic it was on a scale of 1-10 (9), whether the kiss was repeated later (yes), and whether they were still together (no).

The reporter said, "Do you have any advice for the way to make a first kiss memorable?"

Peter thought for a moment before saying, "Make sure you always have breath mints."

She said, "Good one," wrote it down, and the quote ended up in the article.

Everything was a lie, of course. Peter had not been kissed yet. Dante teased him about the article for six months.

7

There's forty-six other apps on the gun," said Dante. He'd worn the military-green duster that he'd found at the Salvation Army before school began. Peter thought it made him look like a Columbine shooter. "We've got to try them all."

Peter watched students streaming past where they stood near the pop machines. "Sounds dangerous to me. What we ought to do is figure out who else visited the dump. Maybe the gun belongs to them."

"You're getting scared in your old age." Dante grinned at a freshman girl as she passed. "Going to school is like a coed buffet. All you can eat, all the time."

Peter couldn't laugh at the joke. It wasn't funny. "Someone's going to hear you say something like that, and you'll regret it."

Dante admired the girl until she entered a classroom. "Maybe you're right and someone is looking for the gun. We should take it someplace else. No sense returning to the spot where whoever owns it might be looking for it. How about the old softball field at Slessing Park? Nobody goes there except pot heads, and that's only at night."

Peter shrugged. "Okay." He knew Dante wouldn't give up until he'd tried the gun again, and he was interested too, even if the memory of the heat waves around the tree before it caught fire were still vivid.

Dante grinned. "Great! See you 5th hour." He pushed away

from the wall and joined the crowd moving toward the classrooms.

Peter worried about strange adults. Suddenly the hall in his
own school seemed threatening. A man in a business suit, carrying a briefcase, walked by purposefully. Probably just a sub,
Peter thought, but the guy looked like he was on a mission,
checking students as they passed him. What would he be looking for? Would someone who used the gun have traces of it
on him? Maybe all the owners would know is that the people
at the dump wore running shoes. He and Dante must have
left footprints everywhere in the clearing. Peter watched his
classmates' feet as they walked by. There were a scattering of
sandals, cowboy boots, and deck shoes, but most students had
running shoes, some of them even the same kind of shoe that
Peter wore.

Another man, wearing a tool belt with heavy pockets and
a hammer stuck in a loop, came out of the janitor's room. Was
that a janitor that Peter had seen before? He couldn't remember. What better way to scope out the students than posing as
a janitor. If Peter wanted to wander through a school without
being noticed, pretending to be a janitor would be perfect.

Or maybe the gun's owner was camped in a van in the
parking lot filled with electronic monitoring equipment. Peter
glanced uneasily at the school's security cameras. It wouldn't be
that hard to hack into their feeds.

I'm just being paranoid, he thought, but when he turned to
go to class, he ran right into Christy Sanders.

"Did you do the reading in *Of Mice and Men*? If you did,
could I borrow your notes?" She smiled, and Peter couldn't
speak. Suddenly it was last night again, except this time she was
right here, physical, immediate. He could smell jasmine—maybe
it was her shampoo—and she was paying attention to him. He'd
never felt so much like a bug under a magnifying glass in his
whole life.

"I . . . umm . . . *Mice and Men* . . . I . . ."

She looked at him quizzically. "Are you okay? You're flushed. Do you have a fever? I tried to do the reading, but someone told me how the book ends, and I don't want to get there."

Peter held up his hand. "Yeah . . . notes." He dug desperately through his backpack, came up triumphantly with the spiral notebook, and almost flung it at her.

"Don't you need them?" she said. "I can give them back at lunch."

"I'm good," Peter gasped out. He could feel the blood in his face. With a force of will, he looked her in the eyes, convinced that if he looked down he'd reveal that he'd seen her, really seen her.

"Okay," she said. "Thanks, I think."

As she walked away, he tried to control his breathing. He imagined his adrenal gland inside his chest—where is the adrenal gland?—pumping all its flight or fight hormones into his system at the same time. His heart hadn't pounded this hard since they timed a mile in P.E.

It occurred to him that today might be a long one.

Until lunch, Peter alternated between studying every strange adult he saw (there were a lot more unfamiliar adults in the school than he would have ever guessed), and hoping that he wouldn't run into Christy Sanders again.

I need to get a grip, he thought. It wasn't like he'd never seen a naked woman. How could he not? He had a computer and access to the Internet. A few months ago he'd wanted some ideas about what to do with the last school vacation, so he searched for "spring break." His screen filled with underdressed bodies.

The Internet gave him an idea, though, so he dashed to the library during lunch to search for information. He looked for images under "guns," "strange guns," —he found multi-barrel muskets from the 19th Century to be fascinating— "multiuse weapons," "unusual landfills," "strange trash," and "unexplained junk yards." No luck. Normally he was pretty good at finding information on the Internet, but today's search was a bust. It didn't help that the school's filtering software blocked half the sites. It didn't like most searches with "gun" in the title. The program was stupid that way. He'd have the same problem if he searched for "breast," even if he was working on a paper on breast cancer, or if he wanted to learn more about breastworks, or if he wanted a recipe for making a dish out of a chicken breast. Half of the human race has them, he thought, but the school administration wants to pretend they don't exist. He shook his head in disbelief.

He could take a picture of the gun, and then use an image-search program to see if there would be a match, but, he thought, if someone was tech savvy and was missing the gun, wouldn't they be on the lookout for a search for the thing they'd lost? His hands froze over the keyboard. Had he already revealed himself by this Internet search? He had logged in under his own name! His search history was practically a confession.

I'm more paranoid than I thought, he thought. He looked around him in the library. The other students were busy at their computers or talking to their friends. No one seemed to be paying attention to what he was doing, but he closed the search program anyway, suddenly afraid that he might already have identified himself as a person of interest. He closed his browser, signed off from the computer, and hurried from the library.

He dreaded 5th period English like he never had before. Dante would be there, and Peter knew that what he would want to do would be to talk about the gun. If they didn't talk about the gun, maybe the gun would go away, he thought, then immediately recognized his own denial. Paranoia and denial, he thought, were terrible in combination, and if he combined that with unresolved sexual feelings, he might well explode. He made a mental note to quit reading pop psychology articles. And, of course, Christy would be there too.

Maybe if he really, really concentrated on Lennie, George, and *Of Mice and Men*, he could get through the class.

Trying *not* to think about a thing only made it worse. Students settled into their desks around him. Backpacks dropped to the floor. Notebooks opened on desks. Pens clicked open, and students talked about their day, but Peter kept picturing the duffle bag revealed from under the sheet of metal. Why didn't he just leave it alone? He imagined the owner of the shoe in the forest, the one who'd left his muddy print, leaning over a computer right now, looking up the class schedule of the student who had searched for strange guns.

Naturally, Mrs. Pickerel put them into groups. Dante wasn't in Peter's group, but Christy was. She and the three other students moved their desks together.

"Thanks for the notes," she whispered in his ear as she pushed her desk next to his, her breath soft on his cheek.

Their discussion topic was "Was Curly's wife a 'rat trap' as George labeled her, or was she as innocent and misunderstood as Lennie?"

Christy slouched back in her chair. "Steinbeck hated women. That's clear. It's not her fault that the men on the ranch saw her sexually and were afraid of her."

The guy to Peter's left who he didn't know well, said, "She knew what she was doing when she went into the bunkhouse and stirred those men up. I'll bet she liked the attention. George was spot on calling her a tramp."

Everyone contributed to the discussion, but Peter stayed quiet, suffering in the irony of a topic about how men see women, and what that says about men.

Somehow the talk morphed into a debate about dating and what kind of person you should date. Two other girls in the group maintained that you should only date someone you love. The guy who'd reminded everyone that Curly's wife was a rat-trap, surprisingly agreed with them, but ruined it by saying, "When you're in high school, though, you date for sex. Love doesn't have anything to do with it. Love is when you're old, like twenty-two."

Christy said, "Girls keep a list, you know, of guys who aren't datable. Your name just went on it." The two other girls nodded, and suddenly Peter wondered if there was such a list. Did girls get together and share notes? That would answer a lot of questions, until he thought of a flaw.

He said, "Then how come so many girls date guys who make them unhappy? If there's a list, shouldn't the bad guys end up alone? From my point of view, they're the only ones who *do* have girlfriends."

Christy laughed at that. "We keep a list, but girls are stupid this way. The good guys end up in the friend zone, and you can't date within the friend zone because it might ruin the friendship. A good friend is more valuable than a boyfriend, so you don't want to risk him. We end up dating from the bad boy list."

"Good for me," said the guy.

"Except for you," said Christy, although it was clear that one of the other girls didn't think so.

"Not *all* girls are stupid," Christy continued. "The smart ones figure out that you have the best times in your life, and you feel more alive and in a better mood when you're with your friend, so eventually, *if you're smart*, you cross a boundary with a friend. That's the only way to go. Friends first."

"Friend zone guys are like brothers," said one of the girls. "Yuck."

"*Like* brothers," said Christy, "because they love you, but they're not your brother. If you can't make that distinction, you ignore the best guys in your life and date the bad ones instead. That's a recipe for unhappiness and abuse."

"Like Curly's wife," said the first girl.

When the bell rang, though, Peter realized he hadn't thought about the gun or Dante wanting to experiment with it for the last fifteen minutes. So, there is a silver lining, he thought.

8

Yesterday's rain stopped before morning, but the clouds remained, hanging low in the sky, heaving their bulk overhead. Peter glanced uneasily at them as he went to the backyard and the Ford his dad was restoring. The old softball field where he was to meet Dante was probably a muddy mess. They'd leave obvious footprints again.

The Fairlane had been sanded to the metal and primed a dull gray. Dad had pulled the chrome off, but the aggressive headlights and retro tail fins betrayed its classic pedigree. Dad told him that it would not be the car he learned to drive in, and that it would be a cold day in hell before he'd let him borrow it for a date. Dad said, "A car like this is just two couches on four wheels. I might just as well give you a hotel room key."

Dad embarrassed him when he talked that way. Dante thought that Peter's dad was cool, however. "My stepdad doesn't have a romantic bone in his body. Good thing Mom didn't meet him first, or I might never have been conceived."

Peter rested his hand on the trunk, checking the area before opening it. He could see the back of his and Christy's house from here, but tall bushes and privacy fences hid the rest of the neighborhood. No one was out, and he saw no movement at the windows. With a deep breath, he opened the trunk. The duffle bag was where he'd left it. Checking behind him one more time, he opened the bag.

The gun was gone.

9

Naturally I have it," said Dante. He sat with the gun on his lap on a splintered bench seat in the home team dugout. Peter was right about the field. The rain had turned it into a pond a half-inch deep. Shiny mud, sticky as clay, made up the rest of the area. If it weren't for the gravel pathways between the fields and to the dugouts, the field would be inaccessible. The outfield had turned into a swamp of knee-high weeds and grass gone to seed. The homerun fences had long ago rotted out, transformed into a sodden tumble of bad wood and faded advertising, and the chain-link that separated the field from the bleachers whose seats were long gone, and that surrounded the dugouts had rusted. Big sections had been bent or pushed down. The old concession stand, a cinderblock building, had one wall that still stood. The rest were reduced to piles of broken cement.

Peter sat beside Dante, dumbfounded. He hadn't even tried texting him about the gun. He'd trudged to the field, playing out how the conversation would go. Either Dante would think that Peter was holding out on him, or he'd blame him for not taking care of it.

Why would someone take the gun but not the translucent bricks? he'd thought. As soon as he saw Dante holding it, he knew.

Dante laughed. "You always hide stuff in that trunk. I ditched

8th period and went by your house to pick it up. I thought I'd get a head start on figuring out its capabilities." He picked up his notebook. "I wrote down the symbol and what it does. We already know about the fire ray and the x-ray. So, try this." He pulled the trigger, which brought the screen up. "Press that one." The icon looked a little like "3lh" all squashed together.

Peter pressed the icon, and the gun clicked in the now familiar way. "What do I do?" he said. Pointing the gun felt like a suicidal act. Anything could happen.

"Aim at that bottle."

A nearly submerged beer bottle poked its neck up near the pitcher's mound. Peter took a deep breath before triggering the mechanism. A thin-lined red crosshair appeared. He centered the sight on the bottle and pressed the trigger a second time. For a second, the gun pulled slightly against his hand. At the same time, the bottle stirred free from the mud and flew toward him. Peter started in surprise. The bottle stopped in mid-air, a foot from the gun. A bit of mud zinged off it when it stopped and stuck to Peter's knuckle. When Peter released the trigger, the bottle dropped to the mud at his feet.

Dante said, "It's a tractor beam. I've already tried it on a bunch of stuff. You can't grab anything too big, which makes sense. If you tried to attract a bus, you'd just lose the gun. It's got to be something small, and it won't work on something too far away." He checked his notebook. "Now try this one." He had copied the symbols that looked like a square made of mostly vertical lines and a broken letter "K."

Peter put the gun in his lap. "Maybe we should turn it in to the police."

"Are you crazy?"

"The police would know what to do with it. Just having it feels illegal to me. We're being stupid."

Dante frowned. "Not stupid. Smart. We found the gun in the dump. Clearly it was thrown away."

Peter thought about how neatly the metal had covered the duffle bag. "Hidden" would be a much better description of what he'd found than "thrown away."

"No, really. Try this button." Dante pointed to the next icon in his notebook.

The gun felt solid in Peter's lap. In *Jurassic Park*, the kids picked up a piece of equipment. Another character said, "Is it heavy? Then it's expensive. Put it back."

Reluctantly, Peter pressed the trigger, found the icon and touched it. The now familiar click within the gun tapped his hand.

"Now point it at the bottle again."

Peter aimed. As before, a crosshair allowed him to pinpoint the bottle. He pulled the trigger, and the bottle flipped off the ground as if he'd kicked it, stopping a foot away, quivering in the air a few inches above the mud. He swung the gun from one side to the other and the bottle moved with it as steadily as if it were attached with a metal rod.

"Aim up and pull the trigger."

Peter squeezed the gun. The handle pushed back into his hand while the bottle took off toward the clouds. It splashed down about where second base would be.

"That's a repulsion ray, I guess. Like the tractor beam, it only works on small stuff, but it can shoot a rock pretty hard. Farther than a slingshot, anyways. I'm not sure what these three functions are. Dante pointed at the next icons on his list. "This one turned the screen black, but the gun didn't do anything. These two gave me a fuzzy screen, like static. Maybe the gun needs a Wi-Fi signal for those to work."

Peter doubted the gun needed anything as prosaic as Wi-Fi. "How many have you figured out?"

Dante counted. "Five that we know for sure. Three that I haven't got yet. That leaves forty more possibilities. I'm hoping there's one that turns lead into gold, or maybe an education ray.

I could choose what I want to learn, point it at my head, and all the knowledge would be there. I wouldn't have to take two more years of Spanish." He laughed, which sounded like the Dante Peter remembered. The one who was goofy and fun. Not the one who told dirty jokes and swore a lot.

Peter pictured the burning tree. "I wouldn't aim that at my head on a dare. Maybe it has a birthday cake setting. I could do with cake and ice cream right now."

A cool breeze that felt more like winter than summer ruffled the water on the softball field. The low-hanging clouds looked like they were ready to soak them again.

"Or a hot chocolate mode. We'd just need a thermos to store it in."

"Wait a minute. I know about the x-ray, the tractor, the repulsor, and the fire setting. That's only four. What's the fifth function we know about?"

Dante took the gun back. Peter buried his hands in his lap. It really was getting cold, and the chain-link fence that enclosed the dugout did nothing to stop the wind.

"Hmm. This may be a hard one to demonstrate." Dante stood, stepped out of the dugout into the mud, and scanned the field carefully. "I need an animal."

"You're not going to kill something are you, like by melting it or blowing it up?"

"Nope, nothing like that."

On the telephone lines that ran along the parking lot, three birds clung to the wire, side by side, a hundred yards away. "How about them?" Peter pointed.

"Good enough, I think. Let's see." He called up the screen, chose an icon, then pointed at the birds.

The gun hummed or whined. Other than the click, it was the first time Peter had heard it make a sound. The birds panicked into flight, fleeing as if for their lives.

"There was a dog when I got here. I aimed at him, hit this

function, and he took off in the other direction, barking like I'd set his tail on fire. Whatever it does, animals don't like it."

A car pulled into the gravel parking lot at the edge of the field. The doors opened, releasing smoke from the inside. Four seniors Peter recognized stepped out. They hung around the convenience store near the school, smoking cigarettes and scaring middle school kids. One of them he knew from when they went to elementary school together, Travis Washington, but he'd been going by "T-Man" for a couple of years. He sat in the back of the room in Peter's sophomore Geography class, smelling like a bad day in a bad bar. It wasn't T-Man's first time in the class. Between the four of them, they didn't have enough credits for one of them to be on course for graduation. They were what the counselors called "super seniors," the kids who wouldn't graduate with their class, if they graduated at all.

Peter and Dante avoided them more from instinct than conscious decision.

"Uh, oh," said Dante as the four boys strode up the path toward the dugouts. "I think we're in trouble. We won't be able to explain this." He looked at the gun.

Peter, trying to act casual, checked around them. The mud would be over their ankles, and if they ran, then the boys would know they had something to hide.

T-Man spotted them, elbowing one of his buddies. His comment was muffled, but the other boys looked at Peter and Dante and grinned.

"Shit," said Dante. "What are we going to do?"

"Bluff it out. Put the gun in the bag." He held open the backpack. "Maybe they'll leave us alone."

"Not much chance of that," said Dante. He pulled the trigger, calling the menu screen to view.

"You can't," said Peter. He imagined Dante turning the four boys into human reenactments of the flaming tree from yesterday. They were only twenty feet away.

Dante brought the gun up before Peter could stop him, aimed and fired.

T-Man and the other boys screamed in terror or pain. Peter couldn't tell. They turned and ran straight for their car, which wasn't at the end of the path but parked off to the side. They splashed through the mud. One of them fell with a huge splash. The others left him to struggle on his own, slipping down again before breaking free. He looked back at Peter and Dante, who kept the gun trained on him, the trigger compressed.

The car started. Gravel shot from the tires as it careened from the parking lot, clipping one of the gate posts on the way. The boy who fell ran after it, water and mud flying from his coat.

Dante put the gun down. "Well, that was effective. Chases off stray dogs and hoodlums. Who would have thought they would have an app for that?"

Peter closed his eyes in relief, letting his weight rest against the chain-link fence.

"I was afraid you were going to burn them."

Dante put the gun in the backpack. "That was my next choice." He met Peter's eyes, and Peter knew that he looked horrified. "I'm kidding. Really."

Peter zipped the bag tight. "I know," he said, but he wondered if he meant it.

10

Late that night, Peter's phone buzzed. The screen glowed like a nightlight in the dark room. He didn't recognize the number on the screen.

"Yeah," he said, after his head cleared enough for him to find the pick up button.

On the other end, someone breathed heavily. The hairs stood up on the back of Peter's neck.

"We know where you live, douche bag. You and your skinny friend." The voice was husky, but not a disguise. Peter recognized T-Man, who sounded like he gargled with whiskey and gravel every morning.

Peter rubbed his knuckle into his eyes, not sure that he was fully awake. "Everybody knows my address. A monkey with an Internet connection can find anyone's address," he said, his voice unusually loud in the silent room. "I also know that if I make a single phone call, your probation officer's going to find out about that pot you sell at the middle school."

There was a pause at the other end. Peter grinned. He might not have a chance against T-Man in a fight, but in a verbal battle, Peter figured T-Man was practically unarmed.

"We're going to turn you and your friend into greasy spots. They'll have to ID your teeth to figure out who you are."

Peter sighed, suddenly happy that he had the strange gun. It was his nuclear option. Maybe turning it into the police truly was a bad idea. "You're boring, T-Man. Idle threats don't worry me, not from a guy who was so scared at the ball field that he had to clean his own underwear so his momma wouldn't see what he'd done in them. I wished I'd filmed it. You and your buddies looked plenty brave tearing out of that parking lot. It'd probably go viral on YouTube. Did the hero you left behind ever catch you, or did he run all the way home?"

He disconnected before T-Man replied.

Once he was awake, though, sleep wouldn't come. After an hour with his eyes wide open, he put on his sneakers and a robe, then went to the Fairlane to retrieve the bag.

In his room, he pulled one of the oddly heavy bricks from the bag. When he shined his desk light through it, the complicated network of gold fibers and tiny squares were visible again. It looked a little like a computer's motherboard, but miniaturized, folded and compressed. No serial number. No logo. No sockets. Just a perfect rectangular brick, about twice the length and thickness of a domino.

He scratched the surface with his fingernail, leaving no mark. A screwdriver in his desk didn't mar it either, and a half hour later, after having hammered, drilled, sanded and torched it with Dad's tools, it still looked fresh and new.

Items he'd kept from the dump lined the long shelf above his door, but he didn't think it would be a good idea to display the brick with them. The stuff on the shelf *looked* worthless, while the brick felt more like a jewel, and he couldn't get over the idea that the contents from the bag weren't thrown away. They belonged to someone. Still, the brick was pretty, and there *were* a bunch more in the bag. One wouldn't be missed. He bounced it in his hand, then, standing on his desk, unscrewed the ceiling vent, put the brick in, and closed the vent back up. That left the hundred or so of the bricks that were in the bag and the gun to hide. He didn't want to leave them in the house, and Dante knew about the Fairlane's trunk.

By flashlight, he went out the back gate in his yard with the duffle bag in hand. This early in the morning, the neighborhood was almost totally quiet. Not even a breeze stirred tree branches. Nothing moved in the alley. His breath turned to fog in the cold air. He opened the gate into Christy's yard, lifting it as he moved it, so it wouldn't squeak. In the back of her property, her dad stored old tools and busted lawn chairs under a carport covered with corrugated tin. During a hail storm, the roof banged and clattered.

Behind a couple of sheets of warped plywood, out of sight from both the alley and the house, stood a rusted barbecue that Mr. Sanders had replaced years ago. Dirt and cobwebs coated it now. It looked like it hadn't been touched in at least a couple of seasons. Peter lifted the lid to reveal a corroded, charcoal en-crusted grill. It was exactly the right size to hide the duffle bag, and it had the advantage of not being on his property. No one would find it here, even if they figured that Peter had it.

11

When he was ten, Dante saved Peter's life. In late April, the days had grown unseasonably warm, and they decided they wanted to jump off the dam into Eaton Reservoir, which was an activity they'd done several times the summer before. Of course, jumping off the dam was illegal (there were signs posted warning trespassers to keep out). Swimming also was forbidden. The reservoir was the town's drinking water supply. That made jumping off the dam even more attractive. In Peter's neighborhood, among the kids, jumping off the dam was practically a badge of achievement. You couldn't hold your head high, walking down the street, unless you'd made the jump.

Peter and Dante were charter members of the jump-off-the-dam club. They'd jumped the first time together. Peter remembered the air rushing against his face as they fell the thirty feet from the top of the dam, and the shockingly hard slap against the bottoms of his feet when they hit, but they'd surfaced laughing, high fiving each other even before they made it to shore, laughing even more because they couldn't both swim and slap each other's hands.

Christy Sanders jumped the next day, along with three of her girl friends. Of course, she trumped them by doing a front flip the thirty feet into the lake.

The heat drove them to try the April jump. Winter seemed to have broken, finally. They rode to the reservoir, towels wrapped around their handlebars. Peter remembered swinging his legs over the rail at the dam's overlook. Dante joined him, both of them letting themselves lean out over the water, holding onto the rail behind them. At the time, nothing seemed finer. The spring sun warmed his shoulders and sent tiny diamond reflections back at them from the water below.

Air whistled by his ears just as he remembered it, and the adventure was glorious until he hit the water. Cold! Like hands of death cold. Paralyzing his lungs. His face burned against the cold. Somehow he surfaced, unable to breathe. Then, finally, a gasp, but it was all freezing water. He choked and went under. Looked up at the surface from a yard below, already losing consciousness. I'm dying. He remembered clearly knowing this was the end.

Then Dante grabbed him. His arm wrapped around his chest and Peter was brought to the surface, brought to the shore, where he lay half in and half out, coughing broken glass from his lungs. Dante lay beside him, gasping from the effort.

They didn't talk about it ever. They rode their bikes home in silence, freezing despite the sun. Peter went to the bathroom, stood in the shower as hot as he could stand it, until the water heater was empty.

He never jumped off the dam again.

Peter saved Dante's life in the spring too, but it was last spring. They walked home from the high school together each day. Devin Avenue was the only busy street they crossed, a four-lane, divided road that grew busy at rush hour, but most of the time was empty, a monument to the city planner's belief that retail would move toward the high school. A half mile farther up the road lead to downtown and the business district, but here there was just a stoplight and the crosswalk.

Dante talked excitedly about a girl he sat behind in math class. "She looks at least eighteen," Dante said. "I hear she's dating a senior who got his last girlfriend pregnant. I'll bet they're doing it."

Peter had been trying to ignore him. This talk about girls and sex stuff had integrated into Dante's conversation a lot lately. Peter tried not to encourage him. He longed for the days when they talked about the movies they'd seen, and the computer games, and books. Although, he was sorry to admit to himself, there was something fascinating about girls and Dante's single-minded obsession.

So, while they waited at the crosswalk on Devin Avenue for the light to change, Peter wasn't watching the light. He was looking away from Dante, to their right. Coming toward them was a white van. Peter remembered thinking at first that a windshield with a crack that obvious in it must be hard to see through, but then he realized something was wrong about the van. It was going way too fast, and it was driving on the wrong side of the street, coming toward them.

The light changed.

Dante, who was saying, "Sometimes she wears these low-cut blouses . . ." as he looked left, and stepped off the sidewalk.

Peter reached, caught Dante's shoulder, and pulled him back.

The van avalanched by, inches from their faces.

A paper caught in the turbulence shot six feet into the air, then drifted like an autumn leaf to rest at their feet.

"Shit, Peter," Dante said. "Shit."

It was the first time Peter had heard Dante swear.

12

One of T-Man's friends was leaning against Peter's locker. Peter spotted him as soon as he entered the hallway. For a second he considered going the other direction, but what could the guy do with all these witnesses? A math teacher stood in his doorway right across from Peter's locker, greeting kids.

The boy looked terrible: circles under his eyes, hair uncombed. Dried mud on his shoes and the cuffs of his pants. He hadn't changed or even cleaned up since yesterday. When he saw Peter, he straightened and took a step back, as if he thought Peter would hit him. The boy's face clenched in conflict. Peter had never so clearly seen someone making a decision in his life, and it looked like one of the choices was to run. He stepped forward, lifted his chin, and waited for Peter to approach.

"Are you a wizard?" he said. His chin quivered.

"What?"

"Or a beast master? I've seen movies, you know. Are you a god?"

Peter decided to let the boy talk his way to sense. "What do you think?"

"At the field, there was that thing." The boy licked his lip, then glanced around as if afraid of being caught from behind. "I couldn't sleep. When I tried, I kept seeing it. We weren't going to do anything to you guys. The ball field's a good place to hang out."

"I know."

The longer he talked, the more miserable the boy seemed, teetering on the edge of tears. "I don't know about T-Man and the other guys, but I'm never going back there. I want you to know that. I don't have any problem with you, so you shouldn't have a problem with me. If T-Man does something, and he might, it wasn't me. I'm not hanging out with him anymore."

"What do you mean that T-Man might do something?"

The boy leaned in. "He's crazy, man. He thinks you tricked us, like with a special effect. An illusion. But it wasn't fake. I could smell it. I heard it breathing. It looked right at me." He closed his eyes as if he could stop from seeing it. "I told him he shouldn't mess with you. I want you to remember that. I warned him, and now I'm warning you. So, don't turn that thing loose on me."

Peter nodded, more confused than anything.

"I'll think about it. Umm . . . thanks for the heads up. About T-Man, I mean."

The boy's face sagged with relief. He shook Peter's hand. "He has a pistol he showed us, stolen from a house he broke into this summer. He brings it to school sometimes. Keep it in mind."

Peter watched as the boy headed toward the gymnasium. He wondered if the gun had a setting that could convert delinquents to productive citizens. That would be an interesting function! But it sounded more like what Dante discovered was a scare-the-hell-out-of-you app.

Peter kept his eyes open for T-Man the rest of the day. He felt like he was in a prison movie. At any moment, T-Man could come up behind him with a shiv, probably a spoon he sharpened in the metal shop, and shove it into his kidney. T-Man wasn't in 3rd period Geography, though, which wasn't unusual. Peter figured he saw him in class less than half the time. He wished he did know T-Man's parole officer. That was a lucky guess on his part. Peter would call him with the pot information on the spot. Better to get T-Man out of the picture before he did anything. The high school would be better without him, and so would the middle school.

Christy met him in the hallway on his way to 4th period. She wore her Pom uniform today, which generally Peter thought didn't do any of the girls any good. The school had backed off of the short, short skirt look this year and gone for sort of a retro '50s thing that dropped the hem lines below the knees, and no matter how hard the girls worked at them, they seemed tailored for people without human figures. Christy, however, somehow pulled the outfit together. Bright red skirt. White, long-sleeved, sweater top with a matching red letter "L" sown in the middle, topped with a red collar. It might be because she wore clothes confidently, which fit her personality, and that when she smiled, most people weren't focused on her clothes.

"Do you have an illuminating moment from *Of Mice and Men* for class? I tried when Lennie talked to Crooks in the barn and Crooks said that all ranch hands had the same dream, but that sounds lame to me, and I have no idea how I'm supposed to turn that into an entire paper. I can't stretch my two-hundred word thought into a thousand-word essay."

The illuminating moment Peter had right then was that he now completely understood a concept Mrs. Pickerel had tried to teach a couple of weeks ago when they were reading poetry: "cognitive dissonance," which she'd explained as being the time when two realities you believed in clashed. On one hand, Christy Sanders wanted to know about their English assignment, a perfectly valid reality that Peter normally would participate in without question. On the other hand, he now possessed a strange weapon with capabilities he'd never heard of that he increasingly was beginning to believe was not a secret government project, but an alien one instead, and that it didn't matter one fig what was the illuminating moment for him in his reading of *Of Mice and Men.*

Christy added, "I could go with Candy deciding that he should have shot his own dog. I might be able to get four-hundred words out of that. After all, I'd have to spend a page or so talking about symbolism and foreshadowing."

Still not thinking about Steinbeck, Peter was happy that he didn't feel like apologizing to Christy as he had earlier, and the blush reflex hadn't kicked in. Then he realized she was waiting for an answer.

He said, "Did you read the Robert Burns poem Mrs. Pickerel assigned? I'll bet I could get a thousand words by claiming that illuminated the novel for me. Throw a poetry quote at English teachers, and they go all weak in the knees. I can probably get her to swoon if I say, 'Wee, sleeket, cowran, tim'rous beastie' with a Scottish accent."

Christy laughed. "Was that truly an 'illuminating moment' for you?"

Peter was impressed he'd come up with this much, but he couldn't sustain it, even at the cost of not making her laugh again.

"I don't know. I just plowed through the reading, most of it during lunch before class. I probably didn't give the book a fair chance. I know how to write a thousand word essay that sounds sincere, though. I think it's my super power."

"You'll have to show me how to do that when I start my paper," she said. "At least you didn't SparkNote your way through the book. It's only a hundred pages long. One of the senior Poms told the sophomore squad to read SparkNotes so they could both stay eligible and make the extra-long practices they'd scheduled for us."

Lots of people Peter knew read the SparkNotes instead of reading the book, which was why Mrs. Pickerel always made up test questions that only folks who'd read the book would get. She was ingenious that way. Peter had heard that she'd given a one-question quiz on *The Natural* to her A.P. Lit class last year, which was, "What happens at Roy's last at bat?" About half the class described—some of them with genuine poetry—how Roy's home run shattered a field light, and that he ran the bases in a cascade of golden sparks from above. Of course, that was how the *movie* ended, not the book, where Roy Hobbs struck out. "Say it ain't so, Roy," said a character in the book.

This was one of the reasons he liked Mrs. Pickerel. For the last quiz, she'd given a true/false test that had a pattern to the answers: two "true," two "false," all the way through the twenty questions. But she had the same class later in the day. She mixed the questions up for that test. About a third of the kids failed because they wrote down the pattern from earlier in the day. Peter enjoyed the idea of how smug the cheaters must have felt as they handed in their tests.

Christy said, "Did you hear they caught an intruder on campus earlier today?"

Peter's eyes widened.

"He was in the counseling office, going through the student records. The secretary saw him and called Assistant Principal Bovine." Bovine was the assistant linebacker coach for the football team, and was larger than any two of his players combined. "Bovine grabbed the guy and called the cops, but he got away."

"Why would anyone want student records?"

"Probably he's a pedophile. Those files have our pictures and home addresses and everything."

"Why not just go through our computers?"

Christy sniffed disdainfully. "My uncle's the IT security guy for the district. He told me that they have military-grade protections for the district's servers. The barriers he's set up against unauthorized use are way hard to get through. Breaking into the student record room where they keep hard copies was much easier. So, do you want to come over tonight and show me how to write a thousand word paper out of two-hundred words of thought? We're having lasagna for dinner. My mom can set out an extra plate."

"That's the draft that's due tomorrow, right?"

"I suppose yours is done."

"Last week. Okay, I'll help," said Peter. "Tonight's the night," but he was thinking about being tracked down. He hadn't, technically, stolen the duffle bag, but he hadn't left it alone, and he hadn't tried to return it either, and he had a suspicion that whoever owned it wasn't likely to give him an award for holding on to it. He was starting to wish that he'd never picked it up. Why couldn't he have just found some more useless junk instead?

13

Peter had never gone on a date. He didn't count the two middle school dances he attended as dates, even though, technically, he asked a girl to both of them. It's not really a date, he thought, if your dad drives you and the girl both ways, and the whole thing takes place before the sun goes down. He wasn't sure what a date would be like, but he was pretty sure he hadn't been on one yet. If there wasn't the possibility of kissing, it wasn't a date.

Both non-dates were in 8th grade. The first was The Turkey Fox Trot and Fall Fling dance. The Student Leadership class decorated the gym with pumpkins, piles of leaves (which continued to litter the halls for weeks after), and scarecrows. Peter asked Loreana Thigpen, who was the tallest student in the 8th grade, easily six inches taller than Peter, and Peter was tall, even then. She didn't dance, and Peter didn't have much motivation to ask her since the girls gathered on one side of the gym, and the boys on the other. The only people who danced were the teachers who sponsored the activity. Also, the whole thing seemed ridiculous since the dance started right after school and was done by 5:00. Sun streaming through the gymnasium windows didn't exactly send a "dance" vibe.

The Mermaids on Parade dance was in the spring. He took Connie Shale who, the first chance she got after Peter's dad dropped them off at the school, showed him a baggie filled with dried leaves that smelled suspiciously like oregano, and asked him if he wanted to "toke up."

Peter went into the gym and didn't see Connie for the rest of the evening. At least for the spring dance, some kids got out on the floor so the teachers weren't the only ones dancing.

He wasn't sure why he was thinking about dates anyway. Going over to Christy's to write a paper about a John Steinbeck novel didn't constitute a date. But there you are.

14

When Peter got home, Dante was sitting on the steps leading up to his front porch.

"Tell me that you moved the bag?" he said. "Otherwise I'm not the only one who knows about the Fairlane's trunk."

"I moved the bag." Peter didn't add where he'd moved it to. He told Dante about what Christy had said about someone in the records room.

"I heard about that. The guy was wearing a blue suit."

"So? Lots of guys wear blue suits."

"It was robin egg blue, like a pastel. Pretty weird if you ask me."

Somebody breaking into the school shouldn't be that big of a deal, thought Peter. It might not have anything to do with them at all. Still, Peter felt the paranoia. "They're closing in, Dante. We need to get rid of it."

Dante looked thoughtful. "What we need to do is sell it. I can post anonymously at one of those Internet markets. We ought to be able to do the whole thing from advertising, to negotiating, to making the delivery and collecting the money without giving away our identities. Maybe whoever it belongs to would be willing to pay for it to be returned."

Peter frowned. "What makes you think that anything you do on the Internet is anonymous? Maybe we should do the same thing, except *not* sell. We should announce where whoever owned it could pick it up."

Dante sighed with disgust. "Goddamn it, Peter. I've got to pay for college in a couple of years, and so do you. If you're going to give away the best go-to-college-for–free opportunities I've ever seen, than you're way more of a fool than I thought."

Peter controlled his voice. He knew he'd been under stress the last two days, and his dad had always told him to talk softly when he was mad. "You think I'm a fool? Who thought that peanut butter on leaves from your backyard would be a healthy food idea? Who picked poison ivy for his little 'eat natural' experiment? Don't call me a fool until you show good sense yourself. This gun, or whatever it is, has disaster written all over it. No joke."

Dante snarled. Peter had never actually heard a snarl from a person before. Dante said, "If you don't want it, then give to me. I'll sell it, take all the risk, and split the profits with you right down the middle."

"I don't think it's salable. You can't just put in on the Internet with a big FOR SALE sign on it like you would an old bike."

Dante slapped his hand on the porch. "And you think the best plan for it is to give it away for free. We *own* it, Peter. We're like those scavengers who search for sunken ships at sea. When they find a ship, they salvage it. They own it if they find it, even if it used to belong to someone else. They get salvage rights. Instead of searching an ocean, we searched a trash heap. Trash doesn't belong to anyone. It's been thrown away. We get salvage rights."

Peter tried to think of a good answer for that argument, but he couldn't come up with one. Dante could be persuasive, and he sounded logical. Nobody throws something away and then gets mad because someone else finds a use for it.

Except, Peter didn't think the bag had been thrown away.

A car turned the corner at the end of the block and headed their way. Peter watched it glumly. He didn't want to argue with Dante, but there was no way they were going to try to sell the gun. Worse than that, though, is he realized that he didn't trust Dante with it. He didn't even want Dante to take it home with him. Peter imagined Dante punching icons at random in his house. The wrong button, and the neighborhood could melt down or blow up or levitate. Peter wondered if there was anything the gun *couldn't* do. Maybe T-Man's buddy at Peter's locker had been right. The gun was no different than a wizard's staff. Maybe it did make them gods. Was there an app that could call down lightning? Was there an app that could turn a person into a toad? Could he raise the dead? Would apps that did any of those things be any more unlikely than what they'd already seen?

The car stopped in front of Christy's house. Christy jumped out of the passenger side, grabbed a book bag from the backseat, and then walked up her sidewalk. She waved. He hesitated before waving back.

"You're the luckiest guy in the school, Peter. What I wouldn't do to have my bedroom window facing her bedroom window."

Peter got up, repulsed. "Give me a break. She's a person, not a peep show."

"A very pretty person," Dante said reasonably. "So, have you tried that x-ray vision app on her yet?"

For the second time in as many days, Peter found himself blushing.

"Not quite holier than thou, are we?" said Dante. "I've got to go to dinner with mom and the stepdad tonight. Let's meet tomorrow to see what else the gun can do."

15

Dad sat in the kitchen, eating a sandwich. He read from his laptop, which was open on the counter, while holding the sandwich in one hand and a glass of milk in the other. People told Peter all that time that he looked like his dad. Dad's narrow face and angular nose made him younger looking than he was. Only the gray hair gave his age away. Like Peter, he was tall and slender, but other than that, Peter couldn't see the resemblance.

"Do you know anything about this e-mail?" Dad asked. "It says it came from the school."

Peter walked around the counter to read the message. It had the school's group mail header. Every parent and student would have received it. WE KNOW YOU HAVE OUR PROPERTY. WE WILL TAKE YOU APART IF IT IS NOT RETURNED. REWARD OFFERED.

Dad said, "All caps is a bit of overkill. Odd wording too, don't you think? Threat and bribe in one. Normally I get notices about upcoming PTA meetings from the school." Dad put the sandwich down. "There's an attachment."

"Don't, Dad," said Peter, shielding the keyboard with his hand. He envisioned his own picture popping onto the monitor. He said, lamely, "It might be a virus."

"From the school?" Dad laughed. "Not likely."

"It's a hack, Dad. The school didn't send this."

The attachment was a picture of a burnt tree. Peter recognized the branch that had exploded, sending the top third of the branches to the ground. It was the tree he'd torched right after he found the gun.

While he was eating his own sandwich, Peter's phone buzzed with a text message from Dante. "Did you see the school's e-mail? You might be right."

16

Over the lasagna, Christy's parents mentioned the e-mail too. Christy's dad owned three hardware stores, but they were hundreds of miles apart, so he spent a lot of time on the road. From his shape, Peter figured he spent much of that time eating doughnuts. The mom, though, was a slender whippet of a woman who ran marathons regularly and helped coach the middle school track team. Peter's dad had said to him once, "If you want a glimpse into a woman's future, look at her mother." From the mom's appearance, Christy would not have to fight off the pounds as an adult.

Peter wondered why he shouldn't also look at the dad to see Christy's genetic inheritance. After all, she could just as easily favor her dad. Peter filled his plate with a second helping. Evidently, worrying about the gun hidden in Christy's backyard didn't affect his appetite. It could be nervous eating, Peter thought. Christy had changed out of her Poms uniform into a button-up flannel shirt and a pair of fuzzy, red pajama bottoms with yellow ducks. It looked more to him like she thought he was coming over for a sleepover instead of a study session. She'd done her hair in a ponytail and scrubbed off her makeup.

The dinner felt surreal. He hadn't been in Christy's house for years, and he'd never sat at their dinner table. What a weird coincidence that that morning he'd gone into Christy's backyard to hide the duffle bag, and now he was in her house for dinner. It felt like fate taking a hand, like one of those stories from mythology where the gods arranged everything.

"Do you think it's a prank?" said Christy's dad. "Some of these kids are too darned smart for their own good about technology. I heard that it doesn't take but an hour or two after they change the password for a student hacker to break the code."

Peter refocused on the dinner. They'd been talking about the e-mail threat. He imagined that Christy's dad pictured a brilliant but bent teenager hunched over a keyboard, wending his way through the heart of the school district's security system. The kid, fueled with Red Bull and Twizzlers, was surely destined for a career in the dark side of information technology. However, Peter knew for a fact that the principal's secretary taped the passwords to the top of a pullout leaf in her desk, and that the student aids copied them to share with their friends as soon as she left the office, which meant that the whole school had them on the same day they were changed. This was low-tech hacking. The system might be well-designed, but the security sucked. The kings of hacking, the kids in the Computer Geek Club, specialized in hitting the keystrokes that made people's screens display upside down, or they changed the auto-correct so that every time someone typed "the," the computer changed it to "boobs." This would alter the opening sentence of Peter's *Of Mice and Men* essay to "Boobs tragedy of *Of Mice and Men* is that boobs men, Lennie and George, never had a real chance to achieve boobs American dream of 'living off boobs fat of boobs land,'" which would strike the Computer Geek Club as the pinnacle of wit since as far as they were concerned, nothing could be more interesting than "boobs land." The surprise was that even with the password being well known there wasn't more obvious computer mischief. The most nefarious plot Peter had heard was to use the password to send e-mails home announcing a snow cancellation the first time the weather changed enough to make the message believable.

There were no geniuses in the Computer Geek Club.

Christy took him to her bedroom to work on the essay. Her mom refused to let him help with the dishes. "Homework trumps dishes," she said. The last time Peter had been in Christy's room, when she was nine, the walls were pink and covered with My Pretty Pony posters. Now, she'd switched to blues and greens, and the posters were of Lady Gaga, Lita Ford, the Ronettes, Joan Jett, Blondie and Heart. She'd hung a beat up electrical guitar over her door. Peter felt like he'd stepped into a Hard Rock Café.

The room itself was large, almost living-room size. Her bed (where he'd seen her before with the gun set to "x-ray") dominated one side of the room, while a desk, dresser and guitar stand, with a much better looking guitar than the one above the door, filled the other. Her desk held a laptop, a copy of *Of Mice and Men*, and a couple books of literary criticism.

"I didn't know you played," said Peter, and it occurred to him that they hadn't really talked for the last three years. They were the definition of "We went different directions." He wondered what she would think of the gun hidden in her backyard.

"Not well," she said, "for all my effort. You've got to hear this, though." She hit a button on her stereo, starting a long guitar solo. After a couple minutes, Peter started to speak.

"Not yet. Just listen." She turned up the volume.

When it finished, and the singer launched into the lyric, she said, "That's Lou Reed's intro to 'Sweet Jane.' Good stuff, wouldn't you say?"

"I don't know very much about music." He tried to think of anything related to rock and roll that might impress her, but he came up empty. Mostly, if he wanted music, he played movie soundtracks. He particularly liked *Pirates of the Caribbean* or anything by Vangelis.

"Welcome to Christy Sander's school of rock." She put her hand on the guitar without picking it up. "I can teach you what

I like about music, if you teach me how to make sense of this stupid book."

"Let me see what you've got so far."

As she'd said, her essay only had two-hundred words. They sat on the edge of the bed as Peter studied her paper. She said, "See, I've written all that I thought. What more is left once you've said what you think?"

Peter breathed easier now that they weren't talking about music. She'd turned the stereo just loud enough so she could identify the songs, which she did as each one started, but not so loud as to distract him.

"When a paper's short, it's either because you didn't support with much evidence, or you didn't explain how your evidence relates to your main idea. See, here . . ." she leaned in so that their shoulders pressed together, " . . . you quoted Crooks, but then you start a new paragraph. You didn't say why you quoted him or how it relates to your argument. You can get another couple hundred words easy. And while you're doing it, I'll bet you can think of other quotes from the novel that are related to what you are saying."

"His quote proves my thesis, doesn't it? It's obvious."

"If it's obvious, why bother writing a paper about it?"

"Hmmm. Good point. So what would I say after the quote?"

Peter thought about how he wrote papers. He hadn't considered his own process too closely. Writing came easily for him. It really was his super power. "Uh, try this. Pretend I'm like twelve. I've read the book. I'm bright, but I'm not sophisticated like you are. You're this cool, smart sophomore, and I'm just a lowly sixth-grader."

"Why, thank you, sir."

"So explain how that quote proves your thesis. I'll show you. I'll type; you say what you would say. Writing's just talking on paper anyways." He moved to her desk, back to the essay on the screen that she'd printed off to show him.

"Okay." She started talking. Peter typed what she said, word for word. She peeked over his shoulder, her hand resting on his arm.

When she ran dry, she said. "That's a lot of typing. How long did we go?"

"Let me read it back to you," which he did. "So, do you sound smart to yourself? I mean, do you sound like you know the book and you've thought about it?"

She smiled. "Sort of. Yeah. I guess I do."

"All your ideas and language. Nothing from me."

"How long is it? How many words do I have left?"

Peter checked the word count, then laughed. "You're at one-thousand three-hundred."

"No way," she gasped.

"Total way."

"That's amazing. I had no idea I knew so much."

"And that's how you turn two-hundred words into a complete essay."

"You're a mastermind." She hugged him, much to his surprise. "On the next essay, I'm going to ask you for help much earlier."

"Do you think you'll need it?"

"Just because I went a few feet without training wheels doesn't mean I'm ready for an entire bike hike. That's a metaphor, by the way."

Peter looked up at her, standing beside him at the computer, and he knew the evening was nearly over. Once they started on the essay, he'd quit thinking about the gun or the ominous e-mail, or what Dante was going to do, or what plans T-Man had. For the last hour he'd been in Christy Sanders' room, talking about homework. Things could hardly get better. Then he had an idea.

"Could you play that first guitar bit again and tell me what I should hear in it? I need to be smarter about music."

She did.

As he walked back to his house in the dark, his hands deep in his pockets against the cold, he thought the evening was way better than a date.

17

Late that night, a rumble woke Peter. He lay on his back, thinking that another thunderstorm was moving over the town, but two dull thumps followed by another rumble didn't sound like thunder at all. He wrapped a blanket around himself before opening his window. It was true that his window faced Christy's, separated by only a low privet hedge and thirty yards of lawn. Her house was dark, though.

On the horizon, hidden by Christy's house and the neighborhood trees, something bright flashed as if a fireworks exploded. He wondered if it was at the high school as another heavy thump rolled over the house. A fire siren sounded somewhere, followed by others. A cop car, emergency signals flashing, raced through the intersection at the end of the block.

Something big is going down, he thought.

A wavering yellow light shone through the trees on the horizon. A fire? Was the high school burning?

The door opened behind him. Peter turned as his dad walked barefoot into the dark room with a blanket around his shoulders too. "Seems late for the Fourth of July."

"Sounds like a war zone."

Dad said, "What do you know about war zones?"

"I saw *Saving Private Ryan* and *Lord of the Rings*. I've got some background."

Another series of thumps, followed by a loud clatter, like

heavy paper ripping. Dad said, "You know that one of those is a fantasy, don't you?"

The echoes of the last sound faded. A light flicked on in Christy's house. Peter guessed there were lights going on in a lot of houses. The sirens seemed to be headed toward the high school. The woods with the dump were on the other side of the school. Whatever was going on could be happening there.

This wasn't the man in a robin-blue suit sneaking around the school, or threatening e-mails. Peter didn't know what to make of it, but Dad was still in the room, and Peter didn't want him to see that Peter was more interested in the night's pyrotechnics than was warranted. What had they been talking about? Oh, yeah.

"I know one's a fantasy. You don't think I really believe in World War II, did you?"

Dad patted him on the head. "That's my boy."

18

The morning news said that police and fire departments responded to a series of explosions and a fire in Melville Park. Peter didn't know that the untended woods beyond the school even had a name. It certainly had never been improved. A copter video showed the clearing where Peter and Dante had explored the dump, but there didn't appear to be a dump there now. Instead, many of the trees were down, and a pall of smoke covered the ground. "Authorities are investigating the cause of last night's disturbance," the announcer said. "A gas line leak or a buildup of explosive gasses in the sewer lines appears to be the most likely cause according to a press release from the mayor's office," she continued. "In the meantime, classes at nearby East High School are cancelled for the day while work crews continue to investigate."

Normally, Peter would celebrate, but the chances that a gas leak caused last night's display seemed unlikely. Why would the gun's owner blow up the clearing? Were there other secrets there that they wanted to hide? Was last night a warning to whoever had the gun?

His phone buzzed. The text message from Dante said, "Meet me at the softball field in an hour. Bring it."

19

The problem with hiding the duffel bag in Christy's yard was that at night it seemed much more secure and hidden than it did with the sun up. From the alley behind Christy's house, three other houses had a clear view of him and what he was doing, and, of course, the back windows of Christy's house also oversaw the carport where he'd put the gun. So, after trying to act casual, he strolled to her back gate, slipped into the backyard and behind the plywood sheets that hid the barbecue. He felt terribly exposed, his nerves on end, and when he held the heavy bag dangling from his hand while trying to silently close the barbecue's` lid, Christy's "Hey, whatcha doing," nearly scared him into a scream.

She stood on the sidewalk beside the carport, holding a garbage can. Dang, thought Peter, I forgot it was trash day.

By the time they reached the old softball field, which was no longer a shallow pond, but still muddy, Christy seemed to have accepted at least a part of Peter's explanation of how a duffle bag ended up in her barbecue.

"This gun, or whatever, among other things, can actually set a tree on fire?"

"Tree, house, whatever. I only tried it on a tree."

"And it might be able to do a bunch of other stuff, but you don't know yet."

"That's why we're meeting at the field. We figure if we're away from people and buildings, there's less chance of hurting anything."

Dante sat in the dugout, scowling, as they walked toward him. Peter couldn't imagine that Dante would be happy about involving a third party.

"What did you tell her?" Dante said as they sat on the dugout bench. His notebook was out, pen ready.

"Nice to see you too, Dante," said Christy. She turned to Peter, "How much *have* you told me?"

"She knows all the functions we've discovered so far." But not everything we've done with them, he thought.

"But you don't know where the gun came from? Let me see it. You might have missed something."

Dante said, "Don't pull the trigger. It's possible that we could cause an explosion. After last night, an explosion is going to attract unwanted attention."

"Peter said you were going to see what else the gun can do today. Did you have a plan for that that *didn't* involve pulling the trigger?"

Peter handed her the gun. She smiled as she turned it over in her hands. "Looks homemade." She gripped the handle and pointed it toward the pitcher's mound. "Did you notice that it's built for a hand with six fingers?"

"What?" said both Peter and Dante. Peter was genuinely startled.

"Yeah, look." She held the gun up so that they both could see. Her fingers dropped neatly into the shallow depressions at the front of the grip, but below her little finger, the handle didn't end. There was one more indentation.

"It could be decorative," said Dante.

"I doubt it. A tool is functional. This looks functional, practical. There's no practical reason to make the handle too long. How did you not notice this before? Can I try it?"

"Sure," said Dante glumly. "Why not? At this rate, everyone Peter knows is going to know about the gun, and we'll have to take a number to have a turn."

"I'm not just anyone," she said. The screen popped into view. "Which icon?"

"Do that one," said Peter. It was the symbol beside the tractor beam function. She touched it. Peter heard the click in the handle, then she pointed toward the pitcher's mound, through the chain-link fence, and pulled the trigger a second time.

Peter held his breath. In the distance, he heard a helicopter, and closer, behind him, beyond the empty parking lot, a car door slammed, but nothing else happened. He half expected a plague of locust to materialize, or the mud to turn to lava. Instead, a September fly buzzed by Peter's head before landing on the rusty fence.

Christy partly lowered the gun and turned toward Peter.

Don't point the . . ." Peter started to say.

". . . gun at me," he finished. Christy and Dante leaned over him, concern on their faces.

"You dropped like a sack of wheat, buddy. Lucky you didn't smack your head."

"Are you okay?" said Christy. "I didn't let go of the trigger. I thought I'd killed you."

"What happened?" Peter shook his head. His ears were ringing a little bit, and when he tried to sit up, his head swam. He lay back down to let his balance settle. "Did I pass out?"

Dante sat on the bench above Peter's head. "Passed out or went to sleep. You were snoring."

"How long?"

Christy checked her phone. "Two minutes. I got pictures. Want to see?" Peter nodded without thinking of repercussions.

He looked peaceful in the picture, but stupid. Mud covered the dugout's floor, and he'd been laying in it. He tried to sit up again, this time without problem. "I'd write 'sleep ray' for that icon. I wonder about its range."

Dante said, "If we smuggled the gun into class, we could put the teacher to sleep. Anytime you were bored, you zonked the teacher, and then did whatever you wanted. The teacher wakes up, you zap her again."

Peter pulled himself up onto the bench. The wooziness was almost gone. He took the gun from Christy, who was saying, "You know what this reminds me of? The flashy thingy from *Men in Black*, except it does a lot more. Do you think there's a flashy thingy app? I always thought that would be a good capability."

"My turn," Peter said. The next icon looked like two stick-figure birds, one above the other beside a left-facing letter "C." With an exaggerated motion, he aimed the gun away from Dante and Christy. "Remember," he said, "alien guns don't kill people; people kill people. Safety first." The gun clicked. A message in the same script as the icons appeared. "I can't read gibberish. Here goes."

For a second, the gun pulled at his hands. He started to speak, then the air in front of the pitching mound swirled, not like a whirlwind, though. Peter stepped back, still pointing the gun. In a ten-foot high circle, a disk on edge, reality smeared as if what he could see in that circle wasn't the baseball field, but a picture of the field in wet paint. The pitcher's mound, the weeds, the trees at the field's edge, ran together as if the painter dragged his fingers through the image around and around.

"What is that?" said Christy. She stepped closer to Dante. Put her hand on his back.

The motion accelerated until it moved too fast to see, turning the image into a solid gray disk.

Then the gray coalesced, resolved itself into a landscape, a surreal hole that started on the weedy infield and ended in another world, a darker one. Mesmerized, Peter walked toward it, aware that Christy and Dante followed.

Dante said, "It's a doorway."

Standing at the edge, Peter tried to process what he saw. A slope rose where the baseball field was flat, and on the slope, apartment buildings or offices leaned crazily against each other, like they'd been shaken in an earthquake. Telephone poles tilted left and right. For an instant, Peter thought dark clouds shadowed the world. Then he saw they weren't clouds at all; they were hills that came from the sky. Hills that impossibly had buildings on them too. There wasn't a sky. Just jumbled structures clinging to slopes and rock to the front, to the left and right and above. The vast, broken cityscape existed in what must have been a giant cave that went for miles and must be miles high, although caves are dark, while here, in the distance behind and above, the light streamed around the hanging hills.

Peter reeled, closed his eyes, triggered the gun. When he looked, he saw that he'd walked through the mud almost to the pitcher's mound.

"Oh, man, that was awesome. Do it again," said Dante. "The icon next to it is almost the same. Choose that one."

Christy shook her head. "Was that another world? Could we have walked into that? What if we did and couldn't return?"

Peter's heart raced. The icon screen showed four more symbols with the two stick-figure birds and an accompanying shape, different from the reversed "C" of the first one. "We won't go in," he said.

The gun clicked. This time no crosshair appeared on the screen. Instead a solid picture of a hand in red, palm toward him, fingers extended (there were six) filled the screen. He showed it to Dante and Christy. "That looks like a 'stop' symbol to me, or at least a strong caution."

Dante disagreed. "Who knows what that might mean to a six-fingered person. The aliens who designed this probably have a whole other set of symbols than we do. Do you remember the 'white flag' scene from the old *War of the Worlds*? The meteor cracks open, and the three guys are trying to decide what to do, so one says, 'Wave a white flag. Everyone knows when you wave a white flag you want to be friends,' so they wave the white flag and the Martians turn them into ashy silhouettes on the ground. A hand, open like that, might mean 'Welcome' or 'Come on in' or 'We'll wash your cat.'"

"We'll wash your cat?" said Christy, her eyebrows raised.

Peter counted the fingers on the hand again. "You think this is an alien's gun now, not a secret government project?"

"It's a theory," Dante said. "Why don't Christy and I get behind something solid, and then you can press the trigger."

That was the last rational event for the rest of the afternoon. Later, when he went to bed, Peter lay on his back, eyes wide open, thinking about life-altering moments. Before today, the only one he'd had that didn't sound stupid, like discovering that Santa Claus was his dad putting presents under the tree at three in the morning, was when his mom died. Eight days before Peter's tenth birthday, Dad helped Mom to the car so they could go to the hospital. He had wrapped the quilt around her that she'd used for the last couple of weeks to keep warm while lying on the couch. They had told Peter that she was "under the weather," but it turned out to be much worse, and she never came home. At the funeral, everyone hugged him and said, "It will be all right," and it did get better. At least the emptiness filled and he quit thinking about her all the time. The world might even seem "all right" again, but it was never the same. That's what a life-altering moment meant.

Peter shrugged, pointed the gun to the middle of the field again, and activated it.

The air vibrated. The gun's handle grew warm while, inexplicably, the gun felt heavier. Peter struggled to keep it from sagging in his hand. He grabbed it with his other to keep it steady. On the field, an orange light appeared and grew larger. Peter's jaw dropped. Just on the other side of the first base line, only fifteen feet away, the world seemed to be peeling away. What he could see of the field unfolded, like a fruit rind pulling from the fruit, like a portal opening before them, but not a round one. It was a ragged hole, growing larger and larger. The size of a tennis ball, then a basketball, then a hoola hoop. On the other side, a landscape bathed in a sickly orange revealed itself. There were tree things: busted, leafless branches hanging broken from moldy trunks. And still, the rent continued to grow, taller than the dugout, burning at the edges. On the ground, on the other side of the boundary between the muddy softball field and the orange landscape, an animal turned its head and looked at him. He hadn't noticed it at first because it too was a rotting orange color. Peter stared, fascinated. It was no larger than a small dog, but it had two strong-looking hind legs, like a frog's, coiled beneath it, and a single leg in front, protruding from the middle of its chest. A single eye studied him from the center or its awful head, a bare, skull-like gleaming orange bone filled with teeth. Then Peter realized there were dozens of them, all focused in his direction.

A wind pressed on his back, pushing him to the chain-link between him and the field. The hole inhaled. Paper scraps tumbled past the dugout, into the orange world.

Christy yelled something, but her words were jumbled in the roar of the rising wind. She and Dante braced themselves against the chain-link, like they were doing vertical pushups. If it weren't for the barrier, the hole would suck them in. The dugout's aluminum roof rattled and moaned. Trees on all sides bent in the torrent.

Peter stared. Beyond the Cyclops dogs and broken trees, beyond what looked like the remnants of a wall and a tumbled battlement, rose a hill. It might have been a half mile away in the orange world. On top of the hill sat a creature, huge, bloated, tentacled. Its appearance hurt Peter to look at. It twisted the orange world around it, like its intents were too irresistible to be contained in real space.

He could feel it turning toward him. If it looked at him, he knew he would be lost. The parts of him that made him human would be consumed by its awfulness. As surely as Peter knew anything, he knew he had to turn the gun off to close the tear it had created in the world.

Ultimately, though, it wasn't an act of will that made him release the trigger. The Cyclops dogs rose off their haunches, immune to the wind, a malevolent pack, and they moved as one toward his world, toward the boundary. Their movement distracted him. For a second, he tore his attention away from the demon on the hill, and that was enough for him to let the trigger go.

A Cyclops dog made it through before the wounded air healed itself. The tornado that had formed behind them gasped into nothing. With a snarl as grating as broken glass, the dog loped away, though the mud, across the field, until it hopped over the broken outfield fence and vanished in the underbrush.

Papers that had been blown against the chain-link fell to the ground. Peter's heart pulsed hard against his chest. He'd always thought the expression "His blood ran cold" was a hyperbole, but he shivered hard for a moment. When he closed his eyes, he saw the terrible creature on the hill, broadcasting illness and hate, and now he was afraid that the creature knew of him, of him personally. To be a thought in the mind of such a beast was horrible to contemplate.

"I won't be able to sleep," said Christy, her voice tight, as if she struggled between speech and a scream.

Dante said, "I don't know what you're talking about. That was wicked cool. What do you think we did? Did we damage the space-time continuum? Did we make a breach into another existence?"

Peter felt an urge to laugh, but he bit it back. It wouldn't be a healthy laugh, and he might not be able to stop himself if he did. "You watch too much science fiction." But Peter watched science fiction too. Who didn't?

"Why not?" said Dante. "We're in a science fiction story now. Ray guns? Tractor beams? X-ray vision? Parallel universes? Science fiction has come to us."

"Why would you open a door to that universe? What use could it possibly have? Surely you wouldn't go there." Peter pictured the Cyclops dogs. Instead of being on the boundary's other side, they surrounded him. They weren't big, but there were so many. They'd take his legs out, and when he was on the ground . . . the image sickened him.

Dante stood, stretched his back. "That was intense. I'll grant you that. My turn." He reached for the gun.

Peter pulled it back. "Didn't you see what I saw?" His voice raised, and he could feel how close he was to losing it. "You can't ever pull the trigger again. We've got to get rid of it. What if I hadn't been able to turn it off? Can you imagine whatever that was coming through that hole, or what if the hole just kept growing? We can't risk it." He clutched the gun to his chest, even as everything within him screamed to throw it away.

Dante backed up, but Christy moved close to Peter and helped him to sit on the bench. "It's going to be all right," she said, but her voice shook too.

Peter rocked back and forth, looking through the chain-link at the baseball field. No evidence of the portal remained. Once again, it was a quiet, cold afternoon. Christy kept her arm around him while he settled down. He felt the warmth of her arm through his jacket. It was the only part of him that felt real.

Christy said, "We've got to know what else the gun can do, or we won't know what we should be afraid of."

Peter closed his eyes for a second. He could see the creature on the hill in his imagination. "We're in danger."

"Probably," she said, "but we need to know more." She pulled on the gun, but he didn't let go. His breathing had begun to settle down. He couldn't hear his heartbeat in his ears anymore. Suddenly he thought he must look foolish.

He gave the gun up. "If there's a red hand on the screen, don't activate it."

"Really," said Christy. Her breathing seemed to be under better control than Peter's, who inhaled shakily. "What kind of safety feature is a red hand anyway? What if you didn't close the portal? That was a world eater on the other side. A red hand hardly seems like enough. Whoever made this ought to rethink the safety standards."

She handed the gun to Dante, who studied the screen, picking his icon. "You guys are freaking out about nothing. Maybe aliens have fights about their second amendment too. 'The right of the people to keep and bear universe shattering portal machines, shall not be infringed,' or something like that."

"You know what I don't get," said Peter, trying to sound normal, "is if whoever made the gun wants it back, and that it's valuable, why it doesn't have a GPS feature in it. If I lose my phone or it's stolen, I have a 'Find my Phone' app that will track it down. The gun has to be more important than a phone. Why can't they just come and get it?"

Christy said, "It could be illegal technology. It *ought* to be illegal. Whoever made it couldn't put a homing signal in it because someone else could find it, like the police."

"Who cares?" said Peter. "They don't have it now, and I'd like to see them try to get it. Having the gun makes you the toughest hombre on the block." He pressed an icon. Pointed at the field. Pulled the trigger.

Christy recoiled, while Peter fought an urge to hit the ground and cover his head. Mud already soaked his back, and he didn't want to coat the front. Nothing happened, though.

Dante put the gun down, disappointed. "I should get to try another. This was a dud." He bent to his notebook to copy the icon and write a note about its properties.

"Not a dud," said Christy. "Look."

The color of the mud and grass on the softball field lightened. The ground crackled softly and hissed. As they watched, frost coated the area in front of them in a rough fan shape, starting from where Dante stood, and broadening as it headed to the trees beyond the outfield. Crystals an inch or two long pushed from the mud, catching the sun in a thousand glisters. A wave of cold rolled toward them.

"It's beautiful," said Christy.

Reflected light illuminated her face. The trees caught speckles of bright sunlight, and the field itself was both unbearably bright shards of light, and vivid, multicolor refractions, like a rainbow carpet.

Peter walked around the chain-link protecting the dugout and onto the ice field, his eyes watering. Ice crystals crackled underfoot. A snapping and shattering behind him told him that Christy and Dante followed. Already, the sun began the process of melting the field. Water trickled back into the ground. Within a few minutes, only the ice in the trees' shadows remained.

Christy and Peter walked home together, the duffle bag hanging from Peter's shoulder. "I'm sorry I took the trash out this morning," she said. "The thing on the hill . . . I don't want that in my head."

Peter didn't speak, but thought about sudden naps, orange monstrosities, and a diamond field that made the sun more glorious than he could possibly imagine.

20

The noon news spent most of its twenty minutes covering the "Disaster at Melville Park." The station's helicopter footage led the broadcast, replaying the downed trees beneath obscuring smoke. An interview with a representative from the gas and electric company revealed no gas lines ran under the park. "Our lines do not explode," the rep said, clearly miffed that anyone thought his company might be responsible. The weatherman showed the radar and satellite images of the town from last night. "Despite rumors that we suffered a 'microburst,' a violent localized storm, the atmospheric conditions make this highly unlikely." The fire chief didn't try to explain what happened, but reported that wet conditions limited the spread of fire to a handful of trees and bushes. In a disappointing development, an info scroll under a graphic about other strange phenomena, the Tunguska event, a meteor airburst in Russion in 1908 that knocked down trees for over 800 square miles, reported that the high school would resume a normal schedule tomorrow.

A loud throbbing rattled the windows in Peter's house. He stepped onto the back porch, a piece of toast in hand. A dull green helicopter passed overhead, followed by three more. He recognized the angry wasp-shape of a military attack copter. The others were fat troop transports moving in synchronized precision toward Melville Park.

He grabbed a coat and his bike and pedaled after them.

At the edge of the practice fields, where the split rail fence separated the school grounds from the woods, a crew of soldiers stretched yellow tape that they anchored with long metal stakes that they pounded into the soft ground on the school side of the split rail fence. Soon, a tape barricade marked the border. A soldier in camouflage stepped back into the tree line and practically vanished. Only because Peter knew where to look, could he see him.

Above the deeper woods, where Peter's secret dump was, the attack copter circled. The other copters weren't visible. Peter guessed they'd landed in the clearing.

He wasn't the only person who'd come to the school to see what the fuss was. He recognized some classmates in the crowd and a couple teachers.

"The radio said the military is taking over," said Mitch Ling, a junior in Peter's Health and Wellness class. "That's not an army helicopter, though," he added. "I'm ROTC. I'll bet it's the CIA or NSA."

"Do you think it's black ops?" someone else asked.

Peter didn't wait for the answer. He ran back to his bike and pedaled to his house, where he retrieved the gun from Christy's barbeque.

The problem was finding a spot where he could wield the gun during the day but not be seen. If someone was looking for the gun, they would watch the crowd. Surely the person who had taken the gun would show an unusual interest in the military's takeover of the dump.

However, Peter knew the old Goodman's Sporting Goods store that closed last spring was easy to get into (some college kids hosted an informal and highly illegal rave there a couple times a month). Its second story rear windows looked over the park. Peter pushed a window open. Busted cardboard boxes, covered with dust filled the room behind him. He tried not to think about rats as he cleared a space for himself.

The icon screen turned on. Peter chose the X-ray function and pointed the gun toward the dump. On the screen, the woods turned into a denuded set of low hills. Peter moved his finger toward the screen, upping the magnification until he found the soldiers. Not unexpectedly (but uncomfortably) they were naked in the screen.

When he upped the magnification, the gun seemed to solidify its position in the air. Peter decided that it was a form of image stabilization. Since he wasn't using a tripod, at this level of magnification the image should be incredibly shaky, but the gun's reluctance to move kept the scene steady.

Some of men patrolled what must have been the outskirts of the clearing. Others pantomimed digging—he couldn't see their shovels—while others appeared to be studying things on tables the screen made invisible. He grunted in annoyance. Seeing the soldiers didn't really tell him what they were doing, although the fact that there were so many indicated the importance the military assigned to the investigation. He had no idea that three helicopters could hold that many men!

He started to release the trigger to turn the screen off, sorry that he'd been careless enough to use the gun where people might see him no matter how cautious he was, when a man at the edge of the screen caught his eye. Peter leveraged the gun so the figure was centered (the gun moved easily up or down and forward and back, but it resisted rotating, which is why he could see the subjects so clearly). The man didn't look like he was with the soldiers. He looked more like he was watching them. He crouched, peering toward them from fifty yards away. Peter pictured the news video from the morning. Whoever the man was, he would be in the trees, difficult to see from the soldier's point of view.

Peter wondered if he could see the clothes, if the watcher wore a light blue suit. Increased magnification didn't reveal who he was. The man's back was mostly to Peter, so all he could tell was the man had black hair. Peter saw more of his butt than he would have liked. Only the tiniest part of the side of his face was visible. Was that the gun's owner? Was he searching for the duffle bag?

Slowly, the man leaned forward, then he turned and looked back at Peter. Not toward Peter: at him. It was if the man could see Peter through the screen as clearly as Peter could see him. Thin lips and a sallow complexion. Indeterminate age: perhaps forty. Narrow, dark eyebrows. Small eyes. Deep blue, piercing eyes, staring at Peter as he stared at him.

Peter released the trigger, closing the screen. From the window all he saw were the tree tops rising and falling to match the hills beneath them. A half-mile away, hidden behind the trees sat helicopters. Dozens of military men worked in the blasted clearing. And, crouching not too far from them, a man who shouldn't have been able to see Peter. He didn't see me, thought Peter.

He kept telling himself that as he rode his bike home. He hid the duffle bag behind a dust-covered toolbox under the workbench in the Ford Fairlane's garage.

21

Christy texted him as he parked his bike. "Come over." She met him at the door. Going to her house the second time in less than a day, after not being in it since her 9th birthday party, seemed strange. They sat at opposite ends of a huge couch in the living room, a respectable room filled with dark leather furniture and bookshelves.

"We need to get rid of that gun," she said. Her eyes were red-rimmed. She'd changed clothes from this morning to sweats and a headband. She always dressed so well at school, as if modeling fashion for trendy teens. Peter found the contrast disorienting. There were two Christys, the one at school who was so popular and out of reach, and this one who reminded him of the girl he used to be friends with.

"That's what I told Dante." Peter started to put his feet up on the couch to face her, but he decided it would be rude. This didn't look like the kind of couch that anyone would sit at that informally.

She did put her feet up. She wore fuzzy blue socks that looked warm and a little childish. "I thought I had a handle on what the world was like. This year I'd keep up my grades—it's not too early to be thinking about college, you know—and I thought maybe I'd get a job on the weekends. Something fun at the mall, maybe, so I'd have spending money. Next year, as a junior, I'd pad my resume with things that look good—I don't think Pom captain as a junior is impossible—and I'd sign up for one of those overseas trips that juniors and seniors can go on. There'd be football games and dances and parties. I'd learn to play the guitar better, maybe even get in a band. By my senior year, I'd have a college picked out, and I'd go out into the real world, ready to be an adult. I thought I knew what the world was like."

Her leg trembled, just a little. She'd wrapped her arms around her knees to face him.

Peter wasn't sure what to say. He didn't know where she was going with this. "Of course you'll be Pom captain."

She shook her head. "No, no, no. You're missing the point, Peter. Pom captain? What would that matter? Didn't you see what was on the hill, on that runny, rotten, molding orange hill? Didn't you see it? Pom captain can't be important after that. The world isn't what I thought it was. Whatever that was wanted to swallow us. It wants to swallow the entire Earth."

Peter had been trying not to think about the monster on the hill. He'd kept himself busy riding his bike and spying on the military so he wouldn't have to think about what he'd seen. Sleep tonight would come hard, and when it did, what dreams might rise?

He looked around the room, at a loss for words. On the wall across the room, a large wardrobe made of dark oak dominated the wall. The bookcases had been built around it.

"Is that an entertainment center?" he asked. "We could watch something to take our minds off it."

Under the big screen TV behind the doors, were two shelves with DVDs on them. His dad liked DVDs too, although Peter hardly played them. He streamed almost anything he wanted to watch, and he was more likely to use a tablet in bed to see a movie than to put it on the television, but his dad was old-fashioned that way, and he liked videos that weren't always available online. "How about something light?" he said.

"I don't care." Christy pressed her forehead against her arms. Her voice was flat, and that scared him more than what she'd talked about. Thinking about the monster on the hill was like standing on a cliff's edge. There was a sickening in the stomach, a lurching in the inner ear, and the vivid image of leaning forward just a tad. What scared him about heights wasn't that he might fall, but that a tiny bit of him wanted to fall. The abyss contains an urge. The image of the orange world and the orange demon was surely a cliff's edge in his head. The key was to stay away from it, to not dwell on the thought.

Just as when he stood on a high place and felt the edge's pull, he could picture himself stepping over. He saw him pressing the two stylized birds icon again, letting the orange world open before him, but this time he would walk forward. The skull-faced Cyclops dogs would move aside. Peter would walk across the orange landscape, past the broken trees and crumbling battlements, until the tentacle being on the hill noticed him (but, of course, it always noticed him—it noticed him even now), and turned its face toward him. Peter could not imagine that face, but he knew that seeing it would melt his brain. He would gibber, he knew. He would go slack-jawed, and drool, and then finally fall, his eyes melting in his skin. He knew exactly what Christy feared.

"How about *Toy Story 2*?" He held up the DVD case.

They sat together in the darkened room. Peter took a blanket from her room and covered their legs. At first she didn't appear to be watching. He couldn't see her trembling, but he could feel it. She sat rigidly, as if her muscles were clenched in a full-body fist. She didn't relax until near the film's end, when she leaned against Peter, and put her head back on the couch. As Woody and Jesse escaped from the plane, just as it took off for Japan, Christy's deep breathing told him that she'd gone to sleep. He watched the ending credits roll without moving. When the screen went black, he still didn't get up. A part of him didn't want to wake her. The other part didn't look forward to going home to an empty house.

His phone buzzed. Trying not to disturb Christy, he slipped the phone from his pocket. Dante's message said, "Check the news. Fake soldiers."

Peter flicked his news app and put in an ear bud. The evening news guy talked in front of an image of military trucks rolling down Devin Avenue. "A mix-up in jurisdiction over last night's mysterious events in Melville Park has caused quite a commotion in the police department. The government investigative unit that arrived this morning in four helicopters, took off about thirty minutes before a second unit arrived in trucks from Fort Franklin. Captain Johnathan Montgomery has taken over operations and is briefing the Chief of Police and fire department at this time. An interview with Captain Montgomery when he arrived revealed the lack of communication."

The trucks rolling into town graphic was replaced by Captain Montgomery standing in front of the City Council offices. A reporter off screen asked, "The government must be taking our little problem quite seriously to send two investigative teams."

The Captain looked toward the reporter, puzzled. "Two?"

"Yes, the first investigators arrived ahead of you this morning."

"This morning?" The Captain bent to say something in his aide's ear. The aide rushed off screen.

"When asked about the makeup of the teams later in the interview," said the newscaster, "the Captain said, 'No comment.'"

22

Late that night, a chorus of howling dogs woke Peter. It seemed as if every pet in the neighborhood decided to let loose at the same time. As he had the night before, he stood at his open bedroom window. City lights illuminated the low lying clouds, rolling across the sky. It didn't feel cold enough for snow, but it wouldn't take much of a change in the temperature to mark the true shift in seasons.

Broad swaths of light from the streetlight out front, and shadows from the trees, striped Christy's yard. Something crossed through a lit space only twenty feet from him, then leaped the privet hedge before vanishing into a deep shadow. The light was bad enough that Peter wasn't even sure he'd seen anything at all. It had been in his peripheral vision, and he didn't get a good look. He strained, trying to make something out of the shadows. The dog across the street barked continuously.

Finally, a shape emerged from the shadow below Christy's window, a black on gray outline he recognized. It was the Cyclops dog. It lay down below her window, seemed to sniff the air, then put its head down on its single front leg.

The neighbor across the street yelled, "Shut up, you stupid mutt!" The animal whined as he was shepherded into the house.

Soon, the other dogs quit barking and the night grew quiet. The Cyclops dog didn't move.

When he texted Christy, she replied, "Let sleeping dogs lie."

Peter went to bed again, but he could see his window, and he kept imagining the Cyclops dog bursting through it. He looked up the number for animal control. They wouldn't start answering their phone until 8:00 a.m.

23

The night should have been over. Too much had happened already, but three hours later, by the red digital numbers on Peter's clock, screaming outside his house and a horrifying, animal growl jerked Peter from bed. Before he reached the window, a sharp series of gunshots rattled the air. A car roared to life on the street, screeching in acceleration as it peeled away, its lights still off.

Just below his window, bathed in moonlight, the Cyclops dog stood, facing the retreating car. The moon's milky illumination gleamed off the dog's bare skull, although in this light, it didn't appear orange. It was a light gray standing on a darker gray, casting a shadow on the lawn. It looked up at Peter. He couldn't see its teeth, but the single eye gleamed.

Across the lawn, on the other side of the privet, Christy's bedroom light flicked on. She stood at the window, a dark eclipse of herself. Peter waved. She waved back. The Cyclops dog did its weird hop-trot across the hedge, and lay down again, as it had before, head on its single front leg.

In the morning, the Cyclops was gone.

The first time Peter experienced altered reality was when he was seven. He'd started reading chapter books instead of picture books the year before. Most of them his dad read to him. He didn't read them on his own. But, for his birthday, his Aunt Janet sent him a three book series by Ruth Stiles Gannet. The first book, *My Father's Dragon*, drug him to another world where a little boy named Elmer Elevator listens to a cat who tells him that a baby dragon needs to be saved.

Peter opened the package along with his other presents and put it aside, but later that afternoon, when the kids had gone home and the cake was gone, and the ice cream that Dad forgot to put back in the freezer had melted on the kitchen counter, Peter opened up the first book, lay on the footstool with his knees on the floor on one side, and the book on the floor on the other, and began reading. There was this place called Wild Island where a mouse talked, and lions were vain, and crocodiles were cruel. The baby dragon had been tied to a tall pole on one side of the river that split the island and forced to give the creatures rides over the water so the crocodiles wouldn't get them. Elmer Elevator was clever. It seemed his backpack held the solution to every problem he faced. He could fool the animals and save the baby dragon, but right at that point, Peter's father came into the room and asked him a question. Peter couldn't remember the question, but he remembered looking up from the book. His living room looked like a strange and alien place to him. The sounds, the colors, the shapes, even Dad felt unreal. It took several minutes to shake off the feeling that his own home existed only in a dream and that Wild Island was the real place.

Reading often affected him that way since then, as did a well-done movie. He remembered looking up from the TV after *The Wizard of Oz* ended, wondering why he wasn't in Kansas anymore.

The path to school felt exactly like emerging from a book or movie, except the sense of alienation lingered. He knew his world wasn't as he'd known it the day before. Everywhere he looked, he imagined the surface peeling like it had at the softball field. He imagined that a hard bump could tear the air aside and he'd see the creature on the hill again who knew he was there. Who wanted him.

When Peter walked in with the kids who rode the bus, chattering away with each other, so concerned about their friends or their homework or their video games, he wanted to shout to them, "The world is not what you believe."

They were the ignorant. He watched two girls laughing at a joke, and he envied them. They lived in a world where jokes mattered. Where the most important question you might face that day was whether to buy the school lunch or run over to the burger joint.

24

At school, all the students could talk about was the military operation in Melville Park. The army had put up their own perimeter tape, but it stretched halfway into the far practice field, and the two guards, guns on their shoulders, looked serious. P.E. classes rescheduled all planned outdoors activities into the gym.

Peter joined a group waiting outside the school library for it to open. Jenny Pearson, a senior, whose mom was a police officer said, "It's a total screw-up. The department has been told to take a hike. Plus, the military guys who were here first took the evidence the department had gathered, and that Captain guy from the second group was furious. He made a scene outside the squad room. Everyone heard."

Tom Tefore said, "My cat's missing." Tom wore shorts and sandals no matter what the weather was, and appeared to own only two shirts: a faded Hawaiian print that said, GO BIG OR GO HOME on the back, and a New York Jets Joe Namath football jersey.

Almost everyone ignored him. He was famous for completely unconnected contributions to conversations, but this time Sean Brolan said, "That's funny. Our cat's gone too."

Miss Zanski, his heavy-set 2nd period social studies teacher whose hair was always done in a bun, joined the students at the door. Peter liked her. She'd let him do an extra-credit report on submarines during the Civil War, even though the class had moved on to the Industrial Revolution. "It'll be nice to get back on schedule," she said to no one in particular. "I don't know what to do with myself when school isn't in session."

Tom Tefore said, "My cat is missing, and does anyone believe that that noise the other night was a natural phenomenon? It was more like a war. Why couldn't it happen again? I don't know why we're in school. We should be evacuating. And my cat never misses its morning saucer of milk."

The librarian walked into view, his keys in his hands. His brown hair hung to the middle of his back and he sported a short beard. Some kids called him Jesus. The sea of students parted to let him through.

As the students crowded behind Jesus, Peter looked over his shoulder. T-Man walked by the crowd. He scowled at them. White surgical gauze and tape covered his left arm, and he limped heavily. When he spotted Peter, he flipped him the bird, although it was clear that twisting hurt his leg.

Peter thought, teach you to mess with a Cyclops dog!

A few minutes after 2nd period started, the intercom clicked and Principal Rappe announced, "Sorry for the interruption, but as a part of the investigation of the day before yesterday's events, the authorities need to touch base with all of our students. This will only take a few minutes. I will call classes to the gym alphabetically. Teachers, if you would bring your roll sheet for today when your class is called, we would appreciate it."

Ray Bean, a scrawny second-year sophomore, immediately left his desk, heading for the door. The last time Peter had seen him move that fast was when he heard they'd brought in a drug sniffing dog to check the lockers.

"Mr. Bean?" said Miss Zanski.

"Uh, bathroom. It's kind of an emergency."

"If you say so," she said. Ray looked relieved as he sprinted from the room.

Principal Rappe called class after class, alphabetically by teacher. Christy, who had Mr. DeMarco for 2nd period, texted Peter. "One guy from the FBI. He knows about the gun! Anyone with info is to talk to him. Reward. He's got a carpet at the doorway everyone has to walk over. Don't know what that is about."

This would have to be the gun's owner, thought Peter. Not FBI either. He texted back. "Might he be the Blue-suit guy?"

"Don't know. Assistant Principal Bovine knows what he looks like, but I don't see him."

Peter put up his hand. "Can I use the bathroom, Miss Zanski?"

At the end of the hall, a line of students, the last class called, lined up at the gym. Peter ducked into the bathroom, found the school's number, and called it. He leaned against the white tile. Next to his head, someone had written in permanent marker: WHERE ARE ALL THE EASY GIRLS? Underneath that, in a different pen, someone else had written, WE'RE NOT TELLING. Underneath that, in a third ink, it said, EASY IS BORING. COMPLICATED IS FUN.

"Can I talk to Assistant Principal Bovine?" he said, deepening his voice. He hoped he sounded older.

"He's out of the building today," said the secretary. "Would you like his voice mail?"

"No, that's fine." Peter disconnected. How convenient, he thought. He wondered if Bovine was tied up to a chair in his house, or something worse.

He texted Christy, "What happened in the gym?"

"Walked in. Sat in the bleachers. He showed a picture of the gun on the wall with a digital projector. Asked us to come forward with info if we had it. Said it was our patriotic duty to help find it. Dismissed us."

"What about the carpet?"

"Black, shiny plastic. Stretched across the door and five feet across. Black box the size of a cigarette pack on one corner."

A student Peter didn't know came into the bathroom. He smirked when he saw Peter texting. "You got to figure out how to do that under your desk. I get and send more texts in a class than I do at home."

"Yeah, thanks," said Peter. He texted, "I should have had you take a picture of the guy."

She sent back a frowny face.

He tried to remember what class Dante had this period. How low in the alphabet was he? "Don't go to the gym" he texted to him. "It's a trap."

"Already been," Dante texted back. "They seemed to have missed me."

"What shoes are you wearing?" Peter held his breath. The far sink in the bathroom dripped. A drop of water plinked against the porcelain every couple of seconds.

"My old tennies."

"What were you wearing at the dump?"

"New Nikes. I haven't cleaned the mud off them."

Peter let out a breath of relief. He looked at his own shoes. He'd cleaned them up the afternoon after they'd messed with the gun the first time. The only thing they had left in the clearing in Melville Park were their footprints. The "carpet" everyone walked on that Christy saw had to be a footprint reader. Peter had never heard of such a thing, but that would be a brilliant way to find whoever had the gun.

For a second, he wondered if he was just being paranoid again. Was it a crime to ditch out on an FBI mandated trip to the gym? It might be, but no way was that an FBI agent.

When Zanski's class was called, Peter made sure he was one of the last students to leave. He followed the line of students, keeping his eye on Zanski. She turned away from them to lock her room. Peter ducked into the janitor's closet, pulling the door shut quietly behind him. An upturned bucket made for a good seat. In the dark, among the detergent smells and old mops, Peter played a deer hunting game on his phone until the bell rang, dismissing class. He slipped out to join the other students and headed for 3rd period.

25

Phoning the police department is like signing a confession, thought Peter—at least if you use your own phone. Caller ID alone would trace a call straight back. Anyone who believed in "anonymous" tips was a fool, at least if he didn't take steps to preserve anonymity. Most of his schoolmates were idiots about information. Half the baseball team was suspended for six games last year because they'd taken pictures of themselves at a beer blast before posting them on Facebook. The third baseman also uploaded a particularly damning video of the rest of the infield and the manager doing keg-stands. The hysterical part of the incident were the cries from the athletes (and many of their friends) that the administration has violated their privacy by viewing the pages. The keg-stand video racked up 250,000 views in ten days.

Peter left the school at lunch and walked to the Walmart a few blocks down Melville Ave. He needed a floppy hat, preferably a cheap one since his wallet was nearly empty, and he didn't want to use a credit card. Swiping a credit card for a purchase was another sure way that someone could find you, if he really wanted.

Fortunately, the gardening department had marked down hats on a rack. He couldn't buy trays of saliva anymore—the season was too late—but the hats remained.

The gas station next door had one of the few public pay

phones left in the city. Everyone had switched to cells. Peter put on the hat and pulled it low over his eyes before walking onto the parking lot. The high-mounted security cameras would only be able to see the hat, not his face. He covered the speaker with a napkin to muffle his voice, then dialed the police. "I'd like to report a possible assault. You need to check on Assistant Principal Bovine's house. He might be in trouble."

He hung up before the dispatcher could ask a question and ditched the hat in a dumpster on the way back to the school.

26

As Mrs. Pickerel wrote historical background for *Of Mice and Men* on the white board, Peter thought about how social media messes with information security. Jenny Pearson, the one whose mom was a police officer, was dating a first-year police officer. Since Jenny was eighteen, and her cop boyfriend was twenty-three, the chat was that her mom wasn't too happy about it, but moms almost always disapproved of their daughter's boyfriend at some time or another. However, the young policeman, in an effort to impress his even younger girlfriend (or maybe he didn't think the information was that important) had been updating Jenny about what he was hearing of the investigation. Jenny, who also didn't think it was that big of a deal, mass-messaged what she learned with her friends, and since everyone else was interested too, facts and rumors spread quickly. The most persistent one was that Captain Montgomery's investigators had found a body. Peter read the text during 5th period, trying out the "under the desk" strategy he'd learned earlier.

Also, the military had ruled out the "bad weather" theory. Chemical residue, shrapnel and other evidence pointed to explosives at the site, which would explain the noise he'd heard that night much better.

Mrs. Pickerel handed out a poem Peter already knew by Robert Burns called "To a Mouse." She said the language was old Scottish, but if students listened they'd understand it perfectly. However, when she started with "Wee sleekit, cowrin, tim'rous beastie" in a really terrible Scottish accent, Peter knew he would be hitting SparkNotes later to refresh his memory.

He glanced over at Christy, who studied her phone under her desk. She turned it so he could see her screen. It was the same message about Montgomery. She looked intently toward Mrs. Pickerel, who had stopped reading to regard the two of them suspiciously. All the while appearing to pay attention, Christy's thumbs flew over her hidden phone. "Was it an accident in the park, or a war?"

"War, I bet," he texted back. "I thought at first that they just wanted to destroy the site, but it sounded like a fire fight. The body confirms it. I'll bet Blue-suit knows."

His phone buzzed again. Dante was looking toward him, so Peter wasn't surprised the message was from him: "We can't get to the woods. Bad guys after the gun. Don't know who to trust. Only option is to figure out the rest of the gun's capabilities."

Peter put his phone between his legs to think. Mrs. Pickerel said, "The poet compares himself to a mouse when he says 'But Mousie, thou art no thy lane.' He says that mice and men are the same. In what way are mice and men similar?"

What way, indeed? thought Peter. None of the poem made sense except the part that said, "The best laid schemes o' mice an' men gang aft agley' which Pickerel said meant that man's best plans often don't work out. Peter wanted to add that even not having a plan didn't work out. It seemed now that no matter what he did with the gun he was in trouble. If he kept it, either Blue-suit, the FBI (or the fake FBI) or the military (or the fake military), or Dante would try to take it. But he couldn't give it away, either. The handful of capabilities they'd discovered so far rendered the device invaluable, and in the wrong hands, who could tell what might happen?

Not having a plan sucked too.

Dante stopped him in the hall on the way to 6th period. Kids passed all around them. He leaned in so he wouldn't have to speak too loud. "You're Bilbo Baggins with the ring of power," he said. "I've been thinking about it, and the reason you're scared of the gun isn't that you think it does bad stuff, but that you think we might take it from you. You're just like Bilbo when Sam offered to carry the ring. You freak out."

Peter took a step back. "You mean Frodo."

"What?"

"Sam never offered to carry the ring for Bilbo. You mean Frodo."

Dante frowned. "Bilbo, Frodo, hobo, who cares. The point is that having that gun is messing you up. Before you know it, you'll be babbling about 'My precious' and eating raw fish from the river."

"That's Gollum. Frodo never ate raw fish. Besides, it's a terrible analogy. The gun doesn't take over your mind. We can be rational about it, and rationality says that we need to keep it hidden until we can give it to the people who'd know best what to do with it. The problem is that Blue-suit is out there, and from what happened in the woods the other night, he's willing to fight for it. I think as soon as he knows who has it, they'll be in awful trouble, whether it's the army or the police. He'll tear through them without slowing. All we have going for us is he doesn't know who has it. He might not even be sure that it's a high school kid. He's guessing because the park is near the high school, and he found our tracks in the mud. He might be desperate."

Peter thought about the FBI guy in the gym. If that was Blue-suit, then he truly was taking a risk. The army was only a field away, and whoever the fake army guys were who came in the helicopters in the morning, they probably hadn't gone away either. What a colossal con job to convince a high school administration to bring every person in the school into his presence! The more Peter thought about it, the more audacious and nervy the move seemed.

Unless, of course, that had been an actual FBI agent this morning.

Christy passed them and waved.

"I'll think about it Dante. Honest. Maybe you're right, but remember, Frodo couldn't share the burden. Everyone knew the ring would destroy them too. Galdalf, Galadriel, Tom Bombadil. None of them took it. You wouldn't want to become Boromir, would you?"

He caught Christy outside of her next class. Even with makeup, he could tell there were bags under her eyes. She probably didn't sleep any more last night than he did.

"Are you okay with, you know, everything?" he asked.

Christy met his gaze. She truly had stunning eyes, a brown so light that they were closer to gold. Peter realized he hadn't looked at them this way before, or maybe she'd never really looked into his eyes before.

"You're sweet to ask. When I woke this morning, I tried to remember what we saw yesterday. Already, the memory is fading some. I'm scared, still. God, I'm scared, but I think I'll get over it. My psychology class said that teens are resilient. The word stuck with me, 'resilient.' It means we can get over stuff. That's why kids who are abused, or whose parents die, or who live through a war, can come out on the other side okay."

"Not all of them are okay," said Peter. He had taken the same psychology class. They learned about post traumatic stress disorder, too, and how some people needed years of therapy to cope with childhood disasters. Not *all* teens were resilient.

"I'm not all teens," said Christy. She touched Peter's shoulder, an oddly intimate gesture for the hallway. Her fingers were warm. "I have seen hell, or at least *a* hell, and I'll survive. So will you. We need to keep telling ourselves that."

The tardy bell rang. Peter hadn't noticed that the halls had emptied.

Christy said, "We have a mission, Peter, to be heroes. We need to make sure no one gets that gun who might open the hole again between that world and ours. If we accomplish nothing else in our lives, we must accomplish that."

27

Peter and Dante played at being heroes from the beginning. In the sandbox when he was eight, Peter built a circular wall around his toy soldiers. He smoothed it with his hands and put grooves in the top so it would look like a castle. When he was done, Dante's men stormed the structure. "We must take the fort," said Dante. They stood outside the sandbox and tossed pebbles like mortars: Peter, trying to knock down all of Dante's men, and Dante trying to breach the wall before his men were down.

The best game they played on the Highline canal, and it lasted several summers. They'd save their allowance to buy model battleships. Dante's porch became a makeshift boat yard. The boys would glue for hours, but they modified the ships to hold firecrackers. Dante's dad kept a shoebox full of Ladyfingers in his closet that he always bought cheaply after the Fourth of July. He never missed the few the boys pilfered.

The point was to put the firecrackers in vulnerable spots in the ship, but not too vulnerable. If the first firecracker destroyed the model, then the fun was over too soon. When they started, they just liked to destroy the ships. They'd light the long fuse, set the boat into the current, and then watch it go down the canal. The fuse smoked enough that the boat looked as if it was under steam, or on fire (it didn't matter). Then the first firecracker would blow. Sometimes the force threw plastic parts into the air, and the battleship continued until the next firecracker blew. The ship listed, more pieces gone. A third explosion deepened the list, and then the boat's bottom blew out, sending the vessel down, stern first. All that remained was a smoky haze on the surface.

But the game became better when they made it a battle. Each boy assembled his ship and placed the firecrackers. By this time, Peter had learned more about fuse length and the best spots to put the firecrackers. He'd learned where to place smoke bombs for better pyrotechnics, and how a well situated pop bottle rocket looked like guns firing (and moved the ship impressively). Dante, too, had become a plastic model demolitions expert. Colored smoke, sparklers, Roman candles. The boats bristled with explosives.

Now the point was to create a war. The two ships sailed into the current, side by side. Each explosion they pretended was a result of a shell from the other ship. The best battles went on for several exchanges, each ship taking more and more damage, but not going down. The ship that was on the surface last won, but only if the remaining fire crackers sunk it too. Both boys had become expert enough to damage their ships but not sink them immediately. A boat that didn't sink wasn't heroic, though. Not sinking meant that you cheated.

The last time they'd played the game, they'd bought big models. Peter went with the Yamoto, a Japanese destroyer, while Dante assembled the Bismarck, a German battleship. The boats were almost two-feet long and had taken a summer of delivering papers to pay for.

"The Japanese and Germans were allies during the war," Peter said as they bought the models.

"Alternate history. In our world, they're enemies. England and the U.S. side with the Germans while China and Russia ally themselves with Japan."

Peter sat on the canal bank, his boat in his lap, admiring the detail in the guns and superstructure. The Yamoto could launch planes, which were glued to its deck. Unlike the other models, Peter had painted some of this one. The longer he worked on it, the more he wanted it to look real.

Dante's version of the Bismarck was equally impressive. He'd done a meticulous job with the decals. It almost seemed a pity to blow them up.

The sun pressed down around them warmly, while the canal whispered at their feet.

"I wish we could film this," said Peter.

"It will be epic." Dante sighed contentedly. School started in a week, but for today, it was still summer. Today they could be admirals. "Let the battle begin," he said.

Peter set the boat into the water gently. They'd lost more than one ship to a careless launch that soaked the firecrackers and ruined the game. "Fire in the hole," he said as he lit the fuse, before sending the boat toward the middle.

Both ships looked so brave, side by side in the canal, heading away from them. The boys walked along side on the road that paralleled the water course.

A sharp crack knocked a hole in the Yamato's deck, sending an airplane spinning away. Flames spurted from the hole.

"Wow!" laughed Dante. "How'd you do that?"

"A little bit of lighter fluid," Peter said breathlessly. He thought about where the other explosions would take place. It was a delicate art to create damage but not sink the ship, and he never knew if the force of a firecracker wouldn't rupture the hull.

The first explosion on the Bismarck ripped away a front gun emplacement, followed by a second near the bow.

"Good shot!" shouted Dante, as if the damage really had been the result of the Yamoto's actions.

More of the Yamoto flew away. Smoke surrounded both vessels as the currents pushed the Bismarck around, almost as if it was lining up a broadside.

Fire had spread to the highest parts of the Yamoto's superstructure, melting the plastic that dripped into the canal. It leaned a little to the side, taking on water from somewhere. Another explosion shook it. Peter imagined his crew manning the guns, fighting for their country and lives, but all of them courageous in the face of the enemy action. There could be no surrender.

The Bismarck vaporized with a huge bang, louder than any firecracker Peter had heard before. Plastic whizzed around him. Something sharp stung his cheek. He was sitting on the road, not even aware that he'd fallen.

Both boats were gone. Only the smoke remained. It eddied away while Peter's ears rang as if the explosion still was going on.

"What was that?" he yelled, his voice sounding small against the ringing.

Dante stared at the water, his jaw dropped. "That was the best, ever," he said.

Peter barely heard him.

"What was that? What happened?"

"Cherry bomb," said Dante. "My step-dad had a secret stash, and now I do too. He's had them since he was a kid. I don't think anyone makes them anymore. Purely illegal. Of course I had to take some. You never know when a cherry bomb will come in handy."

All that Peter knew about cherry bombs was that he'd heard you could light one, flush it, and it would blow up a toilet. "You destroyed your own ship. You lost!" said Peter. "Why would you do that?"

"Both boats were going down," Dante said. His grinned like he'd never stop grinning. "That was awesome. If you're going to sink no matter what, you ought to do it with a bang."

28

Peter sat in a computer kiosk at the public library, a baseball cap pulled low to hide his face from the security cameras, wishing he hadn't thrown away the floppy garden hat. The computer was as far away from the front desk and any foot traffic that he could find. He thumbed through his e-mails on his phone until he reached WE KNOW YOU HAVE OUR PROPERTY. WE WILL TAKE YOU APART IF IT IS NOT RETURNED. REWARD OFFERED, and then copied down the return e-mail address. On the library's computer, he set up a new e-mail account, typed in the address, then wrote YOU CAN HAVE IT. WILL MEET AT THE OLD GOODMAN'S SPORTING GOODS AT 7:00 TONIGHT.

Dante messaged him as Peter closed the computer's browser. Peter ignored it as he considered wiping down the keyboard, thought that was too paranoid, and then did it anyway.

At 7:00, after not replying to three more messages from Dante, Peter retrieved the duffle bag from its hiding spot in his dad's workbench. He punched up the X-ray program, pointed the gun toward Goodman's Sporting Goods, which was over a mile away, and began magnifying. This is an amazing app, thought Peter. The telescope effect seemed infinite. He could continue to magnify anything that the curve of the Earth didn't take out of sight. The more magnification he applied, the more difficult the gun was to move. He wondered if there was a super gyroscope in it to stabilize the image, but the gun was perfectly silent.

The challenge was picking out the store when the gun erased the buildings. He counted streets as he zoomed by naked people in invisible houses and invisible cars until the screen showed what had to be the abandoned store. No one was in it or in front of it (although when he upped the magnification, he could see the building had a rat infestation). Had whomever sent the message not checked for replies? That didn't make sense. They would have been as careful as he was to not be traceable, but they also had to hope someone would contact them. How else could they retrieve the gun?

He backed off on the magnification a tiny bit so he could see more of the area. Luckily, the empty store was in the business district instead of a residential one, and almost all the businesses were closed this late in the afternoon. Not very many people to see. He spotted a naked man on the second floor in the building next door to the sporting goods store, which were mostly realtors' offices. He looked like he was suspended twenty feet above the street. From his motions, he was vacuuming. Also, he needed to get more protein and calories in his diet. A concentration camp victim would have more meat on him.

At the end of the block, near the intersection, another man sat. Peter found it difficult to see people without whatever was around them. Almost everyone seemed to be levitating! From the height, Peter guessed the man was in a car, facing the store. Slowly Peter magnified the image until the man's face filled the screen. Familiar blue eyes and narrow dark eyebrows greeted him. It was the same man who'd been spying on the military operation in the woods. Peter flicked the screen off. He didn't want a repeat of the man looking right at him. The feeling that he'd known Peter was present still spooked him.

The gun went back in the bag, and the bag dropped into its hiding place.

Better to know who I'm dealing with, thought Peter. I know him. He doesn't know me. That has to be an advantage.

He went into the house for dinner.

A small item on the newspaper's online police blotter noted that East High School Assistant Principal Hermann Bovine had been assaulted in his home, suffering only minor injuries. He could not describe his assailant.

29

Dad, wearing a frilly apron that he always wore in the kitchen, fixed macaroni, cheese and bacon, one of Peter's favorites. He asked Peter if the kids were worried about being so close to the site of so much unexplained destruction, and Peter assured him that they were not.

"And how are your grades?" Dad said, toward the end of the meal, even though Peter knew Dad could check his progress online.

"Mediocre to bad."

"You're not going to embarrass the family, are you?" Dad said.

"No worse than grandpa's public drunkenness charge or your counterfeiting scheme. I told you Herbert Hoover wasn't on a twenty-dollar bill."

"Good," Dad said. "Just want to make sure you're maintaining the family's reputation. Don't you go earning any A's. I don't know how we could deal with the shame."

"Got you, Dad. I mostly copy my homework off of Dusty Carmichael."

"Nice choice. Very discerning of you."

Dusty Carmichael was a name the two of them had been using for the mythical worst student of all time since Peter had been in third grade and made the list of "Students of Distinction." Peter had asked if they had a similar list for the worst students in the class. Dad invented Dusty Carmichael on the spot, a student he said had attended school with him, but never risen high enough for graduation from elementary school. "I suppose most kids mistake him for someone's father," said Dad. "Not many third graders shave, you know."

Dad picked up their plates. "I see you hooked up with the Sanders girl."

"Excuse me?" said Peter, horrified.

"Hooked up. You know reconnected. I thought you two had forgotten you knew each other."

"I don't think 'hooked up' means what you think it means."

"I'm sure you are very proper and dignified with her. Dipping her pigtails in the inkwell and whatever else you newfangled kids do nowadays."

"We're not carving our initials on a tree inside of a heart, if that is what you're asking."

Dad wiped the table. "Pity. I always thought she was very cute for a girl with buckteeth like that."

Peter spluttered. Christy's teeth were perfect.

They could have continued the conversation like that for longer, but a knock at the door turned out to be Dante. Peter shut the door behind himself so they stood on the porch. A breeze had picked up, making Peter wish he'd grabbed a coat on the way out.

"I checked your normal hiding places, Peter. No duffle bag. I even checked the fort we'd built in my backyard. No bag. You're not keeping it in the house, are you? If they track us down, going through our houses will be the first thing they do. Give me the bag. I know a place they will never find it."

Peter wrapped his hands around his arms. It truly was cold. Some trees had begun losing their leaves. The wind whipped them across the lawn and skittered others down the street. It had clouded up again. Maybe tonight would be the first snow.

"It's safe." Peter thought Dante looked tense. He'd buried

his hands deep in his pockets and shifted foot to foot.

Dante lowered his voice and moved close. "We need to use it, Peter. We need to go through the rest of the gun's capabilities so we can protect ourselves." A car with tinted windows slid by the house. Peter didn't recognize it, and anything he didn't recognize made him nervous now. Dante said, "We're fools not to use it. We can become crime fighters if we want. We can solve mysteries and help the helpless, but we've got to know everything it can do. Let me have it tonight. I'll go out in the country. My grandma's farm isn't that far away. I can test it in the barn and then tell you what the other icons do."

Peter thought about sharing with him about the man he'd seen in the woods and outside of the sporting goods store, but there was something about Dante's intensity that scared him a little. Peter backed up and put his hand on the door knob.

"I don't think that's a good idea. We're better if we stay out of sight. One of those icons could be a come-hither. You press it and the gun screams for its owner to come save it. I have it in a good spot."

Dante's hands came out his pocket. For a second, Peter thought he was going to grab him, but he retreated instead. "You don't trust me," he said. "You've changed, Peter. You told me once that you thought we were twin brothers of different mothers, but I see now that was a lie. You're just a selfish jerk. It's not yours, you know. I dug as much in that dump as you have. I have as much a right to it as you do."

Peter wished right then that he had the gun on the porch with him. He wished that he could point it at himself and become invisible, if it had a function that could do that, because if he could, he would be able to slip away from Dante and his anger. He wouldn't have to admit that at least in one way, Dante was right.

Peter didn't trust him.

"It's not that," said Peter. "Of course, I trust you. But we have to keep our heads about us. We don't have to rush. There's no way they'll ever find out who has the gun in the first place. I'm sure of it."

"That's bullshit, and you know it. You were never a good liar." Dante stomped off the porch, down the sidewalk to the street. He didn't look back.

Despite the cold, Peter didn't move. His breath felt heavy and dull. He wished again that he'd never found the gun.

Christy crossed her front lawn to Peter's in a gray hoodie top that was too big for her that said CSU ATHLETICS in faded letters on the front.

"Brrr, it's chilly," she said. "What's up with Dante? He acted pissed."

"He's unhappy with me." Peter couldn't think of any more explanation that would capture the moment.

"Can I come in? I've got to show you something."

Peter opened the door for her.

"Hi, Mr. Van Meer. Long time, no see."

Dad typed on his laptop at the recliner. "Good to see you too, Christy. What brings you to our neck of the woods?"

"Peter said he found a good terrorist bomb site. I wanted to check it out."

Dad turned back to his computer. "Okay, but don't blow up anything in the neighborhood. It's terrible for home values."

Peter led her to the back of the house and his bedroom. He wished he'd picked up his dirty clothes from the floor, but she stepped over them without comment and sat at his computer. "I really do have something for you to look at," she said as she typed an address into his browser.

"You could have just sent it to me." Her presence in the room felt unreal, like that painting of an ordinary living room, but there's a mountain floating in the middle.

"We don't have to do everything electronically," she said. "A little face time won't hurt."

"You sound like my dad."

She motioned him over. On the screen, a video was paused. "Daneele Salazar posted this yesterday, after the FBI had us all in the gym. She was goofing around, but watch the background."

Daneele looked into the camera, making faces. First she crossed her eyes, and then she licked the tip of her own nose— Peter didn't know that was possible. Whoever was filming said, "Show us some cleavage, girl." Daneel gripped the top of her blouse closed. She said, "I'm not that sort." The other voice laughed. "Since when?"

"There," said Christy. She stopped the video. In the background, a man in an FBI jacket stood in front of the students, holding a microphone. His narrow eyebrows gave him away.

"I'm seeing him all over the place. I think that's the blue-suit who tangled with Assistant Principal Bovine."

Christy said, "So the question is, is he a good guy or a bad guy?"

Peter sat on the desk's edge, facing her. "Why do you assume he's one or the other? I mean what if everyone is bad?"

"Are you talking about the fake army helicopter guys?"

"Yeah. I don't think that Blue-suit and the helicopter guys are working together. In fact, I'm pretty sure they are not, but what if they're all bad, like rival gangs? We can't just flip a coin and give the gun to one or the other and hope for a fifty percent chance that we chose safely. Everyone who is after the gun might have ulterior motives."

"You mean like Dante?"

Peter paused. On the desk by her had sat a picture of Dante and Peter holding the Little League western region third place trophy. They wore their team hats at the same angle, and had the same smile. Dante had started a double play at shortstop that ended with Peter making the final out at first and won them the trophy. They'd sworn that day that the next year they would be co-captains. Peter's mom died during that winter, though, and he didn't go out for the team the next year.

"Dante's not like Blue-suit."

"But he might have an ulterior motive, right?"

"No . . . it depends on how you define ulterior." Peter could see Dante turning on the X-ray app just to look at girls. The thought of Dante watching Christy in her house—and he was sure that he would—was enough to keep the gun out of his hands, but he wasn't sure that Dante wouldn't open the rift to the orange world just to see again what it looked like, and that was much, much more disturbing. "No, not ulterior, but not safe either."

"What do you mean?"

Peter thought about it for a moment. On one hand, they were talking about Dante, his best friend, or he had been until lately; on the other hand, they were talking about . . . Dante. "He might sink all of our boats."

Christy turned in the chair so that she was facing him. "That's a metaphor, right, like *Of Mice and Men*?"

"I'm saying he's hard to predict. What I'm more worried about are the fake helicopter army guys. I can't believe that they'd bring in so many men to look for the gun, and then take off so quickly. They've got to be around.

"And there's the skull dog from last night."

"I think he attacked T-Man. Did you see him today, bandaged and with a limp?"

"We've got too much to think about."

Peter said, "Maybe we can lay low, do nothing, and it will fade away. If they don't find it, they'll decide they need to look elsewhere, or write it off."

"It won't fade away for me," she said.

"Not me either, I guess. Do you think you'll be able to sleep tonight?"

"Thanks for asking. I hope so. I'm exhausted."

"Me too. Text me, though, if you need to."

She nodded as she got up from the chair. "I'll have my mom

hold my hand if I get too nervous. She'll probably have to hold it for the next month."

Peter couldn't tell if she was joking.

30

The nights have gotten too exciting lately, Peter thought. He'd been trying to fall asleep for a couple of hours, but he couldn't close his eyes without seeing the Blue-suit guy's unblinking stare, or Dante's anger, or the way the air on the edge of the orange-world rift seemed to burn.

Then, a cat outside his window howled and spit, a truly startling sound. It hissed, and then cut off. The silence disturbed him as much as the fuss. He'd never heard a cat's hiss through a *closed* window. He never heard cats. When he opened the window, the clouds covered the moon, so shadows enshrouded his yard. He could barely see the privet hedge between his and Christy's house, but near the middle, maybe on Christy's side of the hedge, something snapped. Peter froze, head cocked to the side. Had he heard that, really? Another snap confirmed it. Crunching. A wet slurping. Then, a familiar growl. It was the Cyclops dog. A shadow detached itself from the other shadows and moved with its distinctive hop-trot toward the street.

He hoped Mrs. Wagner, the retired lady down the block, had brought her cats in for the night. She owned at least twenty. Practically a smorgasbord, if your tastes turned that way.

He wondered as he started to close the window where the Cyclops dog went during the day, but another sound stopped him, a soft swishing hush with a hint of throb in it, like the open heart of a living humming bird held before a fan. It faded to almost nothing, and then a shift below the clouds caught his eye, like the Cyclops dog, a shadow on a shadow, but this one was big, steady and airborne. He followed its curving path a hundred feet above the ground. It was a dark helicopter, criss-crossing the neighborhood. It reversed direction, came directly for him. He stepped back into the room, out of sight, until it passed over the house. He could still hear it, now that he knew what to listen for, and a minute later, he saw it again, nearly silent. If he hadn't have been paying attention, he could have mistaken it for the wind.

He texted Christy, "You sleeping?" hoping that she was. At least one of them could be getting rest, but a message popped back immediately.

"No."

"Helicopter overhead."

Christy's window opened. It glinted against the streetlight. Without her light on, Peter couldn't see her, but he knew she stood there.

"Do you think they know where we are?" she texted.

Peter thought about it. The copter passed by again. "Maybe not specifically. If they knew for sure, they'd be in our houses. Jackboots. Maybe they're scanning." The duffle bag hid under a heavy work table under a corrugated tin roof in his dad's back-yard workshop. He didn't imagine that it would shield a signal very well, although he didn't think the bag sent a signal, or it would have long ago been found. More likely, the helicopter used radar or some other technique to find the bag. If that was the case, the pile of metal boxes and tools on top of the work-bench might be enough to confuse them. Or, it wasn't trying to find the duffle bag. Maybe it was looking for them.

Peter had no idea.

Christy texted, "How do they know to search here?"

"They might not be searching. This might not have anything

to do with us." But he'd never heard of a helicopter that didn't make noise. Somebody who could make the amazing gun could surely assemble a silent helicopter.

The flying shadow reversed direction, came their way again. It *looked* like a search pattern.

A resolve arose in Peter. If they were closing in, then he would have to run. If the Blue-suit guy caught him, and if he really, really wanted the gun, he'd use torture, or threaten his father or Christy. The helicopter guys could be exactly the same. Peter knew he'd never be able to keep the gun's location a secret. The only way to keep it safe might be to flee. He thought about where he could go. It was nearly winter. He couldn't just grab a tent and camp. Surely they would be watching the bus and train station.

A white leaf fluttered past his window, then another. It settled on the lawn, almost glowing. Another one spiraled to Earth closer to Christy's house. Peter found a flashlight in his desk and shined it on the leaf. It was a piece of paper. Watching the sky, he quietly went out his backdoor. The paper was between Christy's and his house, but that was also where the Cyclops dog was. He tiptoed off the porch and to the corner nearest Christy, holding the flashlight stiffly in front of him, ready to flee or throw the flashlight or both. The animal wasn't big, but it had a lot of teeth and a nasty disposition. Trying to keep as much of himself out of sight as possible, he shined the light across the grass. The Cyclops dog lay on the lawn just this side of the bordering bushes, fifteen yards away. It raised its head off its paw to look his direction. Peter almost retreated, but the dog hopped to its feet, turned around, and then dropped to its haunches. It turned its head to the side and studied Peter. The creature turned in a circle again, then plopped back into the same pose, head cocked to the side. He acted like a lapdog, like one of those little balls of fur that old ladies carried in the crook of their arm, except his mouth looked like a moray eel in need of dental work, and his single eye reflected like an orange mirror.

Peter ran onto the lawn, keeping the light on the dog that watched him the whole way, but never moved, grabbed the paper, then made it back in before the copter returned. He wrapped his feet in a blanket when he got to his room. That will teach me to go barefoot in September at night, he thought.

On one side, the sheet said, WE NEED TO TALK TO YOU ABOUT THE BAG AND ITS CONTENTS. The other side had a web address.

A quick text exchange told him that Christy had noticed the papers too. "They dropped leaflets," she texted. "Is it propaganda, like in World War II?"

"I don't know. It's a website. I'm not checking it from home. They might be able to trace an IP address."

So they weren't searching, or they weren't *only* searching. They were trying to make contact. No one except the people who had found the bag would know what the note meant. Everyone else would be puzzled. Peter thought it was brilliant.

The copter sounds retreated, toward the school, still gliding back and forth in long, sweeping lines. They were cruising the city! He wondered if the other copters were up, for full coverage.

This is stupid, Peter thought as he was about to text Christy again. He climbed under the covers and called her instead.

He said, "I've been thinking. They're either secret government agents, aliens, time travelers, or people from an alternate dimension."

"It's the middle of the night," she said, her voice a whisper in his ear.

"You were up anyway. What do you think of this idea: we didn't know the gun existed until I found it. Our lives were perfectly okay before then. Whatever the gun did, and whoever owned it, did it and owned it before I wound up with duffle bag, so if I just made sure that they got the gun, then everything would go back to normal."

"No harm, no foul?" said Christy.

"Exactly. We're off the hook."

"You really believe it might be aliens? You're taking a risk floating something that crazy in front of me. I could decide you were a loon."

"Do you think I'm a loon?"

"No. The truth is out there."

Peter sighed happily. She made an *X-Files* reference! There had to be something intrinsically good in a person who could do that.

She continued, keeping her voice low. Her house was dark, her parents asleep, and she was on the phone with him. Peter padded out of bed, shut his bedroom door as she spoke.

"The problem with that plan is that someone died in the woods. Remember they said they found a body? If someone died, then I'll bet one side or the other will kill again to get the gun. If you offer it to the wrong one, they could kill you after you delivered it. The difference between before you found the gun and after is that before it was a secret, but now *you* know. Not only that, but Dante and I know too. Maybe they wouldn't think it would be a big deal to off three teenagers to make it a secret again."

Outside, mysterious helicopters cruised silently over the city. On his lawn, the devil Cyclops dog was eating the neighborhood cats, in his dad's workshop, a duffle bag containing a gun that could rip open a door into hell waited to be discovered. It was hard for Peter to believe that a week ago his biggest worry was that his sophomore year might be boring.

"You're right. We're stuck and on the defensive. I need a better place to hide the gun, too. If someone figures out I have it, I can't have it on my property."

"Put it back in the barbecue."

"You sure? That might make your risk bigger."

"Only you and Dante were at the dump. You were the only ones who left footprints. No one except your dad and Dante even know that we've been talking more. Can you think of a better place, I mean one that would actually be secure?"

He shook his head. She was right. In theory, hiding something should be easy. The problem was that he couldn't put it somewhere that it might accidentally be found, like in a hollow log or an abandoned building. A burial somewhere could work, if he could get to and from the place with a shovel and not be noticed, but then wondering about if it was safe would prey on him. He could see himself sneaking to the burial spot to see if the dirt had been disturbed, and even if it hadn't, wanting to dig it up.

"I should call the police. Come clean. Let authorities handle it."

Christy laughed. "That would work if it isn't a secret government project. If it is, Blue-suit could just walk in and claim it. He's already pretended to be FBI, or he actually is FBI."

Peter turned over onto his back, phone to his ear. The window cast no light, but his computer, his clock, and his printer all shone like little lighthouses, throwing the dimmest of shadows on the walls and ceiling.

"You know, I've never talked to a girl late at night on the phone."

She lowered her voice to a husky, breathy drawl. "Do you want me to talk dirty?"

Peter stuttered, "No . . . I meant . . . god, no."

"Good," she said. "I wouldn't know how to anyways. Your anxiety is cute, though."

"I'll see you at school," he said. "We need to work on a plan."

"Agreed. Sleep tight."

Oddly enough, he fell asleep easily after that.

31

At dawn, he moved the duffle bag back to Christy's barbecue. The Cyclops dog wasn't there. He wondered again where it went during the day.

It wasn't until he finished breakfast that he realized that although he didn't want Dante to know where the bag was, it didn't worry him that Christy knew.

When Peter was in 1st period, taking geography notes, an office aide came to class with a call slip for him to report to the assistant principal's office. Bovine still had not returned to school (blinding headaches was the rumor), and Dr. Hecke, the other A.P., was meeting with someone, so Peter sat on the short couch in the administrative office's reception area. The secretary had waved him to his seat, but didn't greet him. On the opposite wall, four glum-looking students also sat. He recognized one as a member of the Church of Perpetual Smokers who hung out at the convenience store next to the campus. Peter guessed they were probably here to serve an in-school suspension, which sucked for them.

Motivational posters covered most of the cinderblock walls. He particularly liked the one of a road painting crew standing over the sign they put on the street that read SHCOOL. The caption underneath said, EDUMACATION, YOU SHOULD GIVE IT A TRY. He also attempted to puzzle out exactly the message on the poster that exhorted students to REPORT

DANGEROUS UNDERAGE DRINKING, which implied that some underage drinking was not dangerous. That was news to him.

Dr. Hecke's door opened. The Assistant Principal, a portly, thin-haired woman in her fifties, motioned him in.

"Sorry to get you out of class, Peter," she said. "But our FBI friend wanted to talk to everyone who missed his information meeting in the gym yesterday."

Peter's heart lurched. Blue-suit, in his black FBI jacket sat at the round conference table, a tiny laptop open next to him. His dark eyes darted to Peter for a second, then turned back to his computer. "According to Mrs. Pickerel's attendance yesterday, you were in class, but you didn't make it to the gym." He had a high-pitched voice, like a child's, but there was nothing child-like in his expression or posture. "Why did you miss the gym, Peter?" He looked up, his fingers on his keyboard.

"Uh, I went to the bathroom. By the time I finished, the class was coming back. Someone told me you just showed everyone a picture and asked if they'd seen it. Didn't sound like I could contribute." He controlled an urge to bolt for the door, and his heart pounded in his ears. Stay casual, he thought.

"National security isn't something to miss, son. This is what we're looking for." He handed Peter a picture of the gun that had the now-familiar hand-made look. Peter thought, again, that it was funny that the grip appeared manufactured, but the gun's body was lumpy, like a poorly molded fist. Like a one-of-a-kind piece. That might be its value: that there *wasn't* another one.

"Nope. Haven't seen it." He almost asked if he'd checked the lost and found but decided that sounded flippant. "What's it do?"

"Nothing you need to know. If you see it, though, or hear anyone talking about it, report it to this office. I'll be checking back while we continue the investigation."

Peter leveraged himself up from the chair. "Sure. Good luck finding it." He hoped he didn't sound sardonic as he headed out of the office.

"Oh, Peter. I need you to stand on this first." Blue-suit's voice rose at the end as if he was asking a question. Beside the desk, Blue-suit had set up a black mat on the floor, about eighteen inches to a side. It looked like a miniature version of what Christy had said was inside the door to the gym when all the classes reported, a footprint reader.

Peter panicked, a sick feeling that tore him between fleeing and throwing up. *He knows! He knows!* thought Peter.

"No problem," Peter said, surprised at how steady his voice came out. *He knows! He knows!*

Like a condemned man, Peter stepped onto the mat.

Blue-suit checked his laptop, then said, "You can go."

Peter walked out, trying to appear casual, but his fists were tight. When he got to the hallway, he unclenched to find he'd drawn blood on his palm from his own fingernail.

Then he checked his shoes. The ones he'd worn on the day he'd found the gun weren't what he was wearing. They must still be on the back porch, where he'd cleaned them. He laughed, drawing a glance from a teacher passing by.

In the cafeteria, Jenny Pearson held court. "My boyfriend said there are *more* army trucks in Melville Park. They're not pulling out soon. He also said the police got calls from all over town last night about helicopters, quiet ones, dropping papers. Have you been to the website on that sheet of paper? Nothing on it but a comment box. Pretty stupid stunt if you ask me. Probably an advertisement. And to top it off, people are reporting lost cats, lots of cats. He says we're living at ground-bizarre-zero."

Peter poked at his food, not hungry. Blue-suit had said to call him while "we continue the investigation." Did that "we" mean he had allies in town, or did he say it that way to maintain the illusion that he was FBI? And he still could be FBI. What if he wasn't Blue-suit, and someone else escaped from Assistant Principal Bovine? What if the assault on Bovine wasn't connected to anything at all?

Didn't Bilbo Baggins say once that adventures sucked when you were on them? They were fun to read about, but they were always about the people who made it to the end—those orcs and elves, men and dwarves who were cleaved, stabbed, burned or clubbed to death didn't think much of adventure—and the heroes always seemed much more confident about their information than he was.

Jenny continued talking, but Peter couldn't hear her now in the buzz of the busy cafeteria. Another thought occurred to him. If everyone in town got the slips with the web address, then tons of people would type it into their browsers to see what it was, including bunches of kids from school. He could check the web address and not raise suspicion without resorting to his anonymous use of the public library's computers.

In the computer lab, though, he didn't even have to log in. Another kid from his English class was checking the site. Over the boy's shoulder, Peter could see that Jenny was right. The white page's title read, TALK TO US ABOUT OUR BAG. IT'S VITAL THAT IT BE RETURNED. Underneath that was a comment box. The kid typed in, WAS IT PAPER OR PLASTIC? He turned to Peter, "Paper or plastic? Get it? Like when you're in the grocery store?" The comment box required an e-mail address to be submitted, so the kid typed IAINTTALK-ING@STFU.COM

The height of wit, thought Peter. He wondered what would have happened if the kid typed I'VE GOT IT.

The computer beeped, and a message popped up: NOT A VALID E-MAIL ADDRESS.

32

The sun dropped below the horizon as Peter walked across the lawn to Christy's front door. She answered when he knocked. She put her fists to her hips. "So, did you duke it out with the FBI guy in Dr. Hecke's office, or did you fold under the threat of torture?"

"How'd you know I was in the office?" Peter wondered if she'd sneaked the gun into school and had been watching him.

"Brittany Jones is on the Poms squad and she's the secretary's aid. She told me you looked like a five-year-old with his hand in the cookie jar."

Peter laughed, and it felt like the first time he'd relaxed since he'd found the gun. Christy closed the door behind them. "Let's go to my room. We can talk there."

Her mom sat on the living room couch, reading a magazine. "Sure," she said, "You kids go talk about your young adult things behind closed doors so you don't shock an old fuddy-duddy like me."

Peter said, "Hi, Mrs. Sanders. I heard you ran a 5K a couple of weeks ago that would have made you a part of the varsity on the high school cross country team. I don't think that qualifies you as a fuddy duddy."

"You can't sweet talk a sweet talker," she said, smiling. "Nice try, though. Oh, and I was kidding about closing the door. Keep it open."

Christy rolled her eyes.

When they got into her room, she handed him her backup guitar and said, "If mom thinks we're playing guitar, she won't wander back here. Try this fingering." Peter held the instrument, a beat-up acoustic, awkwardly across his lap. She showed her fingers on the strings of her electric guitar that she'd said was a "Bulldog, modeled after the Les Paul Gibson Junior classic," which didn't mean anything to Peter. Her guitar was black. She slid her fingers up and down the strings, producing a squawk through the little speaker at her feet. "Okay, now strum, like you're scraping toast. Not too hard."

Holding his hand the way she said made his fingers feel as if they were being sliced open. He dragged the pick across the strings.

"Not bad. I think you let up on your little finger. You have to keep the strings against the frets. Try again."

The sound was better this time.

"That's the first chord for the Beatle's 'A Hard Day's Night.' Listen, you'll hear what I mean." She picked a file off her playlist on the computer, filling the room with the song, but stopping it after a few seconds. "Now do it again."

"Don't your fingers bleed?"

Christy shook her head. "Not now. At first, though. Whew! Mom made me quit for a couple weeks so that they would heal up. Now I have callouses. I hear if you start with nylon strings it's easier, but I didn't like their sound as much. So, what did the FBI guy want?" She picked a few notes on her guitar.

"I thought he had me, but he's fishing. When I ditched the meeting in the gym, he noticed. I think he wanted to check my shoes. He had a mini-version of the mat everyone walked over to get to the assembly. It's a good thing I have more than one pair. What's that you're playing? It's pretty."

She ran through the riff a couple of more times, and then sang, softly, "*Hey, Mr. Tambourine man, play a song for me. I'm not sleepy and there is no place I'm going to.*" She played the whole song, her voice barely loud enough to hear. Peter closed his eyes for a second, then realized he didn't want to miss what she was doing with her hands. It was magic. Her fingers moved up and down the strings, jumping from one position to the next.

Peter thought about transcendent moments, a concept they'd learned in English last year: a moment beyond normal, human experience. He felt like he was in one. Christy strummed and picked and sang the words like nothing he'd ever heard before. This is silly, he thought. He'd listened to music, of course, even this song, but it hadn't ever been like this. Songs weren't things that real people that you know could do. They weren't available next door from a neighbor you'd known since kindergarten. Her hair hung down, partly covering her face as she bent over the guitar. How can you get that much sound out of one instrument? How can a few notes and a voice blend like this?

Her hands were strong, competent. Fearless. Moving, it seemed, on their own accord. The tendons on the back of her hands showed her effort. For a second he thought he might weep. Chills ran up and down his back.

Christy played the last note. Her voice trailed off.

Peter didn't speak. He couldn't speak.

Christy laid the guitar flat on her lap. "I've never sung *for* somebody before. I'm sorry. My voice is awful. And that song needs a harmonica. I've got a neck strap, but I haven't practiced with it."

Finally, Peter said, "That's amazing. How long did you say you've been playing? Can you do another one?" He hoped she would play "Mr. Tambourine Man" again. He knew he'd never hear it the same way.

"No, not amazing," she said. "I miss-fingered a couple of times. I can do better, but thanks for saying so. I like this song too. Most people play it on an acoustic. Here's a different one."

She checked her tuning, then picked the first few notes before singing again. Her voice this time stronger and somehow despairing. He didn't recognize the song. It was about a fast car and driving somewhere. The story was good, though, and while she was singing, he decided that "transcendent" was exactly the right word.

When she finished, she said, "Dante called me. He wanted me to tell him where the gun was."

Peter shook his head. In the shadows of her room, listening to her play, he'd forgotten their more serious business. "What did you do?"

Christy strummed another note, but it sounded discordant, not beautiful. "He said you were hogging it, that he should have it because he could keep it safer than you could. He sounded definite about it, like I should just believe him and hand it over."

"So, what did you do?" The idea that Dante would go behind his back this way surprised him. They'd never fought before, like they did the night before on the porch, but Dante always said what was on his mind, or at least he did a year ago, before the two of them started drifting apart. Peter's dad used to call them "a majority of two." If the world went sour, but Dante was his friend, Peter felt fine. If everything in the world looked great, but Dante was mad, gloom and horrifying shadows filled Peter's life. They protected and trusted each other. Sadly, Peter admitted to himself that the rules of their friendship had changed.

"You guys are pretty close, aren't you?" Christy looked uncomfortable. "I feel like I'm getting in the middle of something."

"I don't know him as well as I used to," said Peter. "He's changed a lot in the last few months. Friendship's a flexible state, I guess."

"We're friends, right?" Christy studied her guitar, not meeting his eyes.

"Yeah, I'd say so. Do you want to be friends?"

"Here's the deal," she said. "I don't think I have any."

"Friends?" Peter didn't know whether to laugh or not. The

idea was ludicrous. She was one of the most popular kids at the school.

"I'm not kidding. I used to love *Anne of Green Gables*. Have you ever read that book? It's great—not a boy's book, I suppose—and it has this amazing character in it, Anne Shirley. She's on a lifetime search for a 'kindred spirit.' I like the idea of a kindred spirit. It's somebody who gets you, who you don't have to worry about because they don't have an agenda with you. They just want to be around you, and you want them to be around you too. It's an uber-friend, an ultra-friend. Somebody who I can confide my inmost soul. I don't have one of those."

Peter thought about how it used to be with Dante. Can someone be a kindred spirit temporarily? Wouldn't a kindred spirit be forever? He tried to finger the opening chord of "A Hard Day's Night" while he thought about it. He could get his fingers to the right place, but it hurt. The sound wasn't quite right either.

"I need to tune it. Give it here." Christy took the guitar and played with the tuning pegs.

"What about the Pom team?"

Christy snickered. "Girls can be the most competitive beings on the planet. A couple of them are mad at me for being captain. Another couple think their boyfriends are interested in me. One is sort of in love with me, which makes me sad, and the rest aren't interested in what I'm interested in. And don't ask me about boys, either. What's up with boys anyways? I keep catching them staring at my chest, and everything they say sounds like a come on. And you know what really worries me? That I'm just being full of myself. Maybe none of this is true. The world doesn't revolve around me. I'm not special, but it seems to revolve around me. Have you ever read Sylvia Plath's *The Bell Jar*? That's an eye-opening book. Poor Sylvia Plath spent her whole life pretty sure that men just wanted to sleep with her, and she couldn't decide whether that was a good thing or not. Evidently she didn't believe that she could be both an intellectual human being and an attractive person. Sort of hell for her since she was both."

"Do you think everything I say is a come on?" Peter tried to remember if he'd spent time staring at her chest, and cursed a little bit that she'd said it, because now he was conscious of looking or not looking at her. "I'm a guy."

"That's why I asked if we were friends. Do you think I'm a human intelligence that you like spending time with, or am I a girl who you want to rub up against?"

He tried to pick his words carefully. "That's a minefield question if I've ever heard one. You're sort of both. I mean 'a human intelligence' and 'a girl.'" It seemed that just a few minutes ago, though, she'd been playing the guitar, and he thought of her as a creator of music. He didn't think he had an 'agenda,' whatever she meant by that.

"Fair answer." She mulled it over while still playing with the tuning pegs. "I think it's the sort of answer a friend would make. If you were hitting on me, you'd say something flattering about my looks. I know how this game is played."

"So, if I say you look good, I'm not your friend anymore?"

She smiled. "No, once you're in the friend zone, there are no fouls. I trust you. You trust me. We're safe with each other and we like each other. We're kindred spirits."

"Okay, then. Tentatively, under your definition, I'd say we're friends. Doesn't friendship normally evolve subconsciously, though? I mean, you look at a relationship that's built for a while and you realize that it's the kind of friendship you're talking about? You can't just decide you're friends. You are or you aren't. It's like being in love."

"Another fair point. I'm a self-conscious person. You're a self-conscious person. If you get two people together who think about who they are, who are introspective and self-aware, I think that they could have a conversation like we're having."

Peter let out an appreciative "Hmmm." This didn't sound like any conversation he'd heard in a movie or read in a book before, but it seemed reasonable. "Okay, but I don't think we should have this conversation again. It makes me feel gicky. If you get too analytic about a thing, you can kill it. It's like Mrs. Pickering with that 'To a Mouse' poem. By the time we finished counting the syllables and summarizing the verses and identifying every fricking literary technique Robert Burns used, the poem died. The first time I read it, I thought the whole mice and men are similar idea was cool, but by the time we finished, I think I would have pulled my plow around the field a few more times to see if I could turn up mouse nests that I'd missed. If I don't hear that poem for fifty years, it will be fine with me."

She handed the guitar back. "That's funny! The way you talked about the poem in class, I thought you'd decided it was the best thing you'd ever read. You sounded smarter about it than she did. I'm not kidding. A couple other kids thought so too. How'd you get so smart about literature?"

"How'd you get so good on guitar?"

Christy's dad poked his head in the room. For a big guy, he moved quietly. Peter didn't even know he'd been in the house. "Something's going on outside. Have you heard anything about it?"

At the end of their block, under the streetlight, a large, canvas covered army truck parked next to the curb. Two soldiers cordoned off a section of the street behind the truck with traffic cones and yellow tape, and then set up on a folding table what looked like a small satellite dish. Christy, Peter and a couple of neighborhood adults gathered at the edge of the tape.

"What you boys up to?" asked a middle-aged man wearing a jacket that was too small for him and decorated with lavender fur trim. Peter guessed that it was his wife's jacket.

One of the soldiers, a woman who didn't look much older than Christy, said, "Just a security check, sir. Standard operating procedure. Nothing to worry about. We'll be gone in the morning."

Peter wondered what would happen if he trotted around Christy's house, retrieved the duffle bag and handed it to the soldier. It would be an *easy* solution. He also wondered what would happen if instead he used the gun to peek inside their truck. Were there other men in the back? Were they studying an array of monitors connected to the little satellite dish? Maybe they were monitoring cell phone calls. Maybe they could listen into the nearby houses.

It's not fun being paranoid, he thought. The tension returned to his neck and shoulders. He could feel the relaxation leaking away. It would be so simple to believe what people told you, particularly authority figures, but he'd never been able to do it.

Two people stood under the porch light at his house, facing the door.

"Isn't that Dante?" Christy said.

Peter stopped and grabbed her arm. "He's with Blue-suit."

The dark-eyed, FBI (maybe fake) guy knocked on the door. Peter's dad opened it, but Peter couldn't hear what they said. It looked like Blue-suit shoved Dante when they went in.

He stood on the pavement, stunned. "Dante gave me up," Peter said. "Or he got caught somehow and Blue-suit made him talk. Come on!"

Without looking to see if she followed, Peter ran toward the army outpost on the corner, cutting across a lawn when the traffic cones and tape blocked the path. He heard Christy running behind him. He turned left, past the corner house, around it, and then into the unlit alley. When he got to his own yard, he ducked to stay out of view until he reached Christy's backyard and her gate.

"What are we doing?" Christy said, not out of breath at all. She seemed to have inherited her mother's running stamina.

"I need to see what's going on."

"How?"

Peter pushed the plywood off the barbecue and retrieved the gun. He punched up the X-ray app. "I can see through walls with this."

Inside his house, Dante and Dad sat side by side, their hands on their laps, in Peter's bedroom. Blue-suit moved about quickly, searching the closet, and then his dresser.

"Let me see," said Christy.

Peter handed her the gun. "They'll be naked."

"Yes?"

"Naked. This app erases everything except the ground and animals. Great if you're hunting. No trees to block your view, but they won't be wearing clothes. Thought I'd better warn you."

Their faces were only inches apart, crouched behind the plywood so that anyone looking out Peter's windows wouldn't see them.

"You didn't tell me about that app."

"It didn't occur to me."

Christy shook her head before pointing the gun at Peter's house.

Peter said, "Oh, I've seen you naked with the gun. It was an accident, I swear." He held his breath. He hadn't planned to tell her right then. The words sort of burst out.

"Big deal. I've seen you naked too. What's Blue-suit going to do when he can't find it?"

"Search the rest of the house, I'd guess, but Dante will tell him about my dad's Fairlane, so they'll come out here too. I've got an idea, though." He took the gun back from her. Checking Blue-suit's position, Peter left Christy's backyard and entered his own. Moving fast, keeping his eye on the action on the screen, he stopped at his back door. "How could you see me naked? You've never had the gun."

"What makes you think that?" Christy tried the doorknob. It twisted easily. "You should lock your doors, you know. Anyone can come from the alley to your house. Mom and Dad have two deadbolts on ours."

"Sure. I'll talk to Dad about it later. But you'll notice the bad guy came through the front door, and Dad let him in. Locks wouldn't have helped." He checked where Blue-suit was one more time, then closed the X-ray app, brought up the menu, and pressed another icon. "The plan is, we go in and put Blue-suit to sleep."

"Then what?"

"That's as far as my planning has gone. We can talk about it while he's unconscious."

She nodded. "Your bedroom window faces mine."

"Excuse me?"

"You wanted to know when I've seen you naked. I didn't need the gun. Your bedroom window faces mine. Most people wear a towel when they get out of the shower. You don't. I suppose with just you and your dad, you don't think about it."

Flabbergasted, Peter said, "Your bedroom window is always draped!"

"That's because yours never is. Are we going to do this, or what?"

He opened the door, grateful that Dad hated squeaks. The hinges of every door in the house were regularly lubricated. The kitchen and hallway floor, though, creaked if you didn't know where to step. Not that it would have mattered. Blue-suit was shouting. "Where else would he have hidden it? I don't have time to mess with you two. I get my property back now or life becomes ugly for you both."

Peter took a deep breath, stepped into the doorway with the gun raised, and pulled the trigger. Blue-suit didn't even have time to look surprised before he crumpled. Both Dante and Peter's dad fell backwards onto the bed.

"Shoot. I didn't think the focus would be so broad."

Clothes and books lay on the floor everywhere. The closet

had been cleaned out. Dresser drawers hung open.

"You only slept for a couple minutes, Peter. That's the default. Let me try something." She took the gun from him, and studied the menu screen for a moment. "Like any good app, these have adjustments. Ah!" She swept her finger up the screen. "Duration control."

Before Peter could react, she pointed it at the sleepers and pulled the trigger.

"What if it's a depth control? The lowest setting is a nap. The higher setting is a coma."

Her expression became impatient. "I don't think so. I've been working with the gun a bit. The apps' controls are consistent. Distance, width, height, intensity, duration. There's adjustments for all of them. I already knew about the X-ray app, by the way. It's a Peeping Tom's godsend."

"How would you know how to work the gun?" Astonished, Peter reevaluated the device in her hand.

"You left it in my barbecue. You don't think I didn't get curious? Dante gave me a copy of the apps you've used. I certainly didn't want to try a new one! Did you know that burning down the tree was a fluke? Move the controls a bit, and you could have just drilled a hole as big as a quarter in it. Go the other way, you could have set that side of the glade on fire, or incinerated a single tree a hundred feet behind the rest of the forest. You can set where an effect will occur, even if your view is blocked."

"You got curious? Sheesh!" Peter bent over Blue-suit, who was snoring. "That doesn't sound like a coma. I've got the next step in the plan, now."

"Call the police?"

"Yeah, but you and I will be gone when they get here. Too much to explain. Besides, I think they believe Blue-suit is FBI. We'd lose the gun to the cops, and the cops would give it to him. There's no way they'll listen to us." While he talked, he typed on his computer, bringing up the Internet address from the flyers dropped from the helicopter the night before. In the comment box, he said, "I have the gun. Need to talk." He typed in his own e-mail address. Almost immediately, a chat box opened. The message read, EVERYONE KNOWS WHAT THE GUN LOOKS LIKE. WHAT ELSE DID YOU FIND WITH IT?

Peter typed, A BLUE DUFFLE BAG

WE'RE ON THE MOVE

Peter gasped. "I knew they were tracing the Internet. Nobody's privacy is secure anymore."

Someone pounded on the front door.

"No way they're that quick," said Christy. "Is there?"

He looked at his Dad and Dante, snoozing on the bed, but he couldn't think of a way to get them out of the house.

"Run," he said.

As they went through the back door, the front door crashed open.

Behind the plywood-sheet screen in Christy's carport, Peter flipped on the X-ray app again. Dante, Peter's dad and Blue-suit were where he'd left them, but another man was in the room, his back to them. When he turned, Peter did a double take. The man looked exactly like Blue-suit. Same dark eyes and narrow eyebrows. They could be twins.

"We're not safe here. There's more than one Blue-suit, and we can't depend on Dante not having told them about you. They could be in your house next."

Christy pulled her phone out of her pocket. "I'll call the police now. They aren't going to threaten my mom and dad."

"Do it on the move. We can't stay this close."

They trotted down the alley, away from their houses. The bag weighed heavily in Peter's hand, and being in the open in the daylight, carrying what everyone seemed to be looking for struck him as the height or foolishness.

Christy finished her call.

"We can go to Goodman's Sporting Goods and wait it out

there," Peter said. "Watch out for the army guys with their little satellite dishes. Who knows what their deal is, or if they're authentic or not."

"It's Friday. The rave gang might be at Goodman's, setting up. We won't be private."

"All the better." Peter wiped his brow. The clouds might be low and the breezes wintery, but he'd built up a sweat. "If there's a crowd nearby, we could be safer."

By the time they reached the building, sirens sounded in the distance in the direction of their houses.

"Hope that's the police," Christy said.

The entered the abandoned store through the broken window in the back that Peter had used earlier. Noise and laughter from the front of the building told him that Christy was right. The college kids were setting up for a rave.

The building's back stairs took them to the second-story offices. Outside, evening had started to settle in, shrouding the rooms in shadow. Old desks stacked with broken boxes pushed against the wall leaned uneasily, and when he and Christy cleared off a spot on the floor to sit, a scratching behind the boxes reminded him that he'd seen rats in the building earlier.

He checked his e-mail from his phone. The latest message read, POLICE AND MILITARY AT YOUR HOUSE. EVERYONE SAFE. WHERE ARE YOU?

Peter thought that was interesting. They'd found his home address immediately from his e-mail, but they weren't tracking his cell phone. They might not be as resourceful as he feared. MEET ME IN THE ALLEY BEHIND GOODMAN'S SPORTING GOODS. ONE PERSON ONLY, OR I WON'T BE THERE.

They replied. CONDITIONS ACCEPTABLE. FIVE MINUTES.

"Christy, you get the bag. If you stand to the side of the window, you should see me, but they won't see you. If they take me, or anything looks hinky, get downstairs and mix in with the ravers."

"This is your basic, 'Stay back ma'm' scenario. We both ought to meet them."

"No, it's just logic. The Blue-suits knew I found the gun, and these guys know it too, but they might not know about you. You're the reason I can meet with them. If it was only me, I wouldn't get within a mile of them. They could grab me and I'd be telling them where the gun is in ten seconds. I'm a wimp about pain. My dentist just has to say he's going to fill a cavity, and I wish I had nationally sensitive information that I could trade with him instead."

Christy laughed, but she looked worried. "Tell them up front you've hidden the gun. That way they won't just conk you on the head."

"That's the plan." He tried to look confident, but he was sure she could tell he was shaky. Going down the stairs to the back door, he thought of all the choices he had instead. He could decide to go back upstairs, convince Christy that this was a bad idea (which he didn't think would take much convincing—it *was* a bad idea), or he could head to the front of the building and vanish into the college crowd. Whoever was coming probably knew what he looked like, but he'd be hard to find in the dark of a shoulder-to-shoulder rave.

He put his hand on the door and stepped through.

A security light at the building's corners illuminated the alley, but it was a harsh brightness that created deep, black wells where it didn't penetrate. Only a handful of yards beyond where he stood, Melville Park trees rose like solemn sentinels.

A figure came around the corner, walking briskly. Peter resisted the urge to look up to see if Christy was watching.

It was a woman wearing a long raincoat, belted across the middle, and an old-fashioned man's hat. His dad had one. A fedora. She stopped ten feet away. The far light made her features sharp. He guessed she was in her mid-thirties. The way she walked and the way she held herself made him think she was athletic. There was a litheness to her movements.

"You're Peter Van Meer, I assume," she said, her voice clipped, authoritative.

"Who are you?" Peter checked behind him. If someone else appeared, he planned on dashing for the door.

"Case Officer Wheeler. I'm the commander of the delegation that's come to retrieve the object I understand you claim to have." Her hands were behind her back, which, among everything else, made Peter nervous. "It's hazardous, son. You'll be glad to be rid of it."

"No, I mean what are you? You clearly aren't the army, since you cleared out when the real army came. You've been out of sight for days, except for your stealthy helicopters. Who are you? Where did you come from? Who'd I zap unconscious at my house? And, most importantly, where did that gun come from? It does stuff I didn't think was possible."

She stepped toward him, her business-like demeanor cracking. "We know you activated it. We can tell when it's turned on, and the tree you burned down in the glade showed where you were. You didn't try it more, did you? It's dangerous beyond your comprehension."

"Where did it come from? Who are you?"

"It doesn't matter where I came from. What's important is that I retrieve the bag."

"I don't even know if you're the good guys. I'm not telling you anything unless you give me some answers. There's more than one party after it, and there's a reward offered too."

Wheeler smiled grimly at that. "You wouldn't like how they'd pay you, once they had it. I don't know what you mean by good guys, but they're definitely a bad crowd."

Peter wrinkled his forehead. "Do you mean the two I left at my house? Two doesn't make a crowd. How many are there?"

"You say there were two at your house?" She spoke very fast, but not to him, like she was on a phone that Peter couldn't see. Three men burst from the trees of Melville Park, rushing toward them.

Peter turned to run, but they were already there as the world went black.

33

Christy looked down at Peter, concern written large on her expression. She held a damp cloth that she used to wipe his brow.

"Do I have a fever?" said Peter. He felt loggy and stupid. In the background, a heavy bass beat thrummed, while a red gauze shrouded the ceiling light, filling the room with a macabre light.

"I wasn't sure what else to do," she said. "You weren't waking up. I'm not much of a nurse."

"Where am I?" he said, struggling to sit up, which sent the room swirling, so he flopped back down. "Did you zap me?"

"I didn't see any point in running if things got 'hinky,' as you said. I had the gun. Turns out that it has a good range. We're in a college dorm. I got a couple boys from the rave to carry you out. I told them you'd had too much to drink. They'd had too much to drink too, so they didn't ask why we were carting you off but leaving the other people in the alley. One of them actually said, 'I'll never be so drunk that I'd pass out on the street, man. You've got to be responsible about it,' and then he drove us here. Except when those guys came out of the trees, that's the most scared I've been in my life. Don't ever drink and drive. He was so worried about a DUI that he stopped for *green* lights."

The second effort to sit up worked much better. The room hardly swam at all. He discovered they were on the floor between two single beds in a space wide enough for two small study desks to fit side by side. Hooters girl posters covered the cinderblock walls, and it took a minute before Peter recognized that the lump on each bed was a sleeping college guy.

"Did you zap them too?"

"Nope. They've been out since we got here. I think that one," she waved at the guy whose arm hung out far enough that his knuckles brushed the floor, "spent some quality time praying to the porcelain god before he zonked. The other one was our driver. He's surprisingly strong. Carried you two floors up. Oh, you might have a bump or two on your head. He cornered well but didn't compensate for the wider load."

The bass beat in the background faded, grew stronger, and then sounded like it was outside the door, before fading again.

"What's going on with the music?"

Christy got up, put the washcloth on the back of a chair, before gathering both of their coats. "They have a sound system and a keg in the elevator that they're taking floor to floor. Doors open, you get a beer. I thought the college had rules about drinking in the dorms, which is what I asked our driver when we got here, but he said the student resident advisors are manning the keg. That's why we took the stairs. They don't mind dorm kids drinking, I guess, but outsiders are verboten. I met one of the advisors. He's too drunk to even be in charge of an elevator. We should take the stairs too."

"Do you have a plan for where we're going?" Peter took his coat. "If we stay here, at least no one will know where to find us."

"I'm planless, but this room stinks and I don't think much of their posters."

They shut the door behind them. Many of the other doors were open. The elevator wasn't the only source of music. How anybody could study under these conditions was beyond him. He understood why his teachers said that in college you spent many of your study hours in the library. The dorms, clearly, didn't lend themselves to contemplation.

"You might have shot too soon, not that I'm sorry you did, but I think I surprised the woman from the helicopter squad—her name is Wheeler, by the way—when I told her that more than one Blue-suit was at my house. It sounded to me like one of them wasn't there when they got there. The folks you zapped might have been coming to help, not that you would know that. I didn't find out anything else, other than she's very worried we might mess with the gun. She said it was 'dangerous beyond comprehension.' That doesn't sound good."

"How did Wheeler explain herself to the police and the army?"

They exited the dorms. Peter led them toward the Student Union, holding his collar tight against the wind that pushed the trees shadows into waving arms in front of the campus's sidewalk lights. "Didn't get that from her. If Blue-suit has everyone convinced that he's FBI, she probably can sell herself as CIA or NSA or something. Interpol, for all I know. They're definitely operating under different rules than we are."

At the Student Union in the expansive cafeteria, Peter bought hot chocolate for both of them from a bored coed who never looked up from her Econ book while manning the cash register. They took a table in the corner. About half the tables had students sitting at them, studying, most with jackets and backpacks. After experiencing the dorm, he understood why students weren't hitting the books in their rooms.

His phone buzzed, letting him know he had an e-mail. SORRY FOR THE MISUNDERSTANDING. WE MUST MEET AGAIN. YOUR RULES. YOUR TIME AND PLACE.

Peter typed back, I WANT ANSWERS TO MY QUESTIONS. NO MINIONS.

AGREED.

COLLEGE STUDENT UNION, NOW.

Peter showed Christy the exchange. "Same plan as before.

Scoot to the other side of the cafeteria, cover the bag. Act like a college student. If things go south, slip out the back door."

Christy looked doubtful. "If I shoot from there, a hundred people are going down."

"I don't think it will happen that way again. She didn't give me the same vibe as Blue-suit."

"If we're depending on vibes, then I know we're desperate." Christy took the bag and her coat to an empty table.

Peter didn't see Wheeler coming before she slid into the empty chair.

"Where's your partner?" she asked.

"Far away from here. You've had time to get answers from that guy who forced his way into my house. What's his deal?"

Wheeler shook her head. "I'm afraid we haven't had much luck with him. He's . . . uncooperative. High motivation. He has unforgiving coworkers. And here's a problem, as I found out before your partner fired on us. One of them got away. It's certain he's tracking our moves. We can't stay here."

Across the room, Christy's head was down, pretending to look at her phone. Peter didn't see anyone else who seemed out of place. If Wheeler had brought help again, they hid themselves well.

"You better talk fast, then. I know you're not from around here. Tell me a story."

Wheeler sighed. In the better light of the cafeteria, she didn't seem as harsh, and she was older than Peter had thought at first. "If I'm tracked, and I know I am, then you've just been spotted. We have to come to an agreement, or as soon as I leave, you're exposed."

Peter scanned the cafeteria again. Nothing unusual he could see inside, but the walls were floor to ceiling windows on two sides, and the night hid whatever watched.

He took a deep breath while thinking it through. "It doesn't matter. I don't have the duffle bag. If a Blue-suit gets me, the bag gets away. So you might as well tell me what's going on."

"Blue-suit?"

"It's what we've called them. One of them tried to get to the school records. He was wearing a robin-egg blue suit."

"Robin-egg blue is an unusual color for a suit?"

"Yes, of course. He stood out. Don't switch the subject. You promised me answers."

"You won't understand most of it, and knowing it won't do you any good. What you do know is that a lot of people are interested in what you have, and they won't stop until they get it. You're not safe. Your family is not safe, nor are your friends. It's entirely possible your existence is not safe. The stakes are high, Peter."

"Tell me what you can. What I don't understand could hurt me, so I want to know what we're involved in. The gun, it's not a government project is it? You aren't an American agent. Are you a human one?"

The woman flinched. She reappraised him. "Interesting guess. Closer than you might think. Yes, I'm human, sort of, a neighbor to human. Probably nothing you could detect short of a DNA test, and maybe not even then. We could be exactly the same. Do you know about parallel universes?"

Peter smiled. Oddly enough, this felt like familiar ground. "Of course. Who doesn't? The gun kind of gave us a hint the concept was possible." He could picture the air folding back on the orange world and its monstrosity.

"That's our technological advancement. In almost everything else, we're similar to you, but we made a discovery that opened doors for us. Many bad ones. We've been paying for it ever since. Your gun and the contents of the duffle bag are the result of that mistake. A group, the 'Blue-suits,' took advantage of the technology to find more technology."

"Like having three wishes from a genie, and making your last wish a wish for more wishes?"

"Yes, exactly. While the people I work for have now limited the opening of doors, the Blue-suits have broken laws to gather the most powerful discoveries from all the versions of the universe they've visited. They've made a supertool. Your gun is a crude version of it. A one-of-a-kind experiment, and you've got it." She tapped her fingers on the table, struggling for words. "It's like just one person had a nuclear weapon. We don't want anyone else to get it. Everyone could be destroyed. Not just us, either. They could use our door-opening capacity to move to other universes. They could spread the destruction everywhere. We've locked some doors. They can't get again what they have now. If we eliminate the bag here, it's over."

It's a good story, Peter thought. She's right about the nuclear bomb analogy, but how could he know she's not the one who would destroy worlds?

Wheeler said, "Do you have a way of communicating with your partner? If we can't settle things here, you don't want her to contact you again. You and I leave together, they'll follow us, assuming we're going to the bag. It's the only way to protect the package. We're being watched. I don't have enough men to make this meeting secure. We don't know what they look like."

"Are you kidding? They're clones. They all look like the guy you got at my house. How many of them are there, anyway?"

Wheeler furrowed her brow. "We think there are just three. Clones? What are you talking about?"

"They are exactly the same. The one you didn't get is a copy of the one you did."

The agent pushed herself away from the table. "Contact your partner. We know the one we caught. You saw his twin brother. No clones where I come from."

"They were brothers?" Peter, feeling like an idiot, decided to take a chance, then texted Christy. WE'RE LEAVING. DON'T FOLLOW. DON'T RUSH OUT. DON'T GO HOME.

"Can they intercept my cell phone?"

"We couldn't," said Wheeler. "Give us another couple days and we'll have it. I admire your instincts, though. You have a remarkable sense of self preservation. Come on. It's time to go."

"Oh," said Peter, "let me see your hands."

"What?" Wheeler looked around the cafeteria. "We don't have time for this."

"Indulge me," said Peter.

Wheeler put her hands on the table. The nails were neatly trimmed, and she had twelve fingers.

"Ah," said Peter. "That answers that question."

"Are we done?" asked Wheeler.

Peter didn't try to catch Christy's eye as he followed Wheeler out.

They crossed the courtyard in front of the Student Union, into the empty parking lot. Peter pirouetted, trying to see beyond the parking lot lights in all directions. He bumped into Wheeler, who had stopped. "We need a pickup," she said.

"Are we carrying something heavy? I can't even drive a car yet."

"Not that kind. I wasn't talking to you."

A heavy whoosh from overhead stirred paper scraps on the asphalt into action. A stealth copter landed ten yards away.

Inside, a thinly padded bench was all for him to sit on. He searched for a seatbelt as the craft lifted. He couldn't hear any more that a white-noise hush from the propellers with the doors closed. Wheeler studied him from the opposite bench. Peter said, "Um, the real army is looking for you, I think. They've set trucks up all over town."

"Your radar can't detect this craft."

"It didn't look like radar. I think they were listening posts."

A blinding light shone through the helicopter's window, and Peter pitched hard against the door. His stomach felt like it was trying to leave as the craft turned hard and lost altitude. The pilot yelled back, "We're spotted. Hang on."

"Listening posts? That's cunning." She turned to the pilot. "Get us away from town. They're picking up your prop wash."

"Ground control says they've launched something, coming our way. Might be a jet. We can't outrun a jet."

"The jet won't find us unless we stay where they can keep a spotlight on us. Get us out of town where they can't hear us and can't light us up."

Christy texted, LOTS OF COMMOTION. ARMY TRUCKS IN THE PARKING LOT. SOLDIERS EVERY-WHERE. CAFETERIA IN LOCKDOWN. WE'RE SIT-TING ON THE FLOOR UNTIL FURTHER NOTICE THEY SAID. PACKAGE HIDDEN. ARE YOU OKAY?

He didn't like it. In the confusion, the Blue-suits might go after Christy. They'd talked to Dante, and if Dante mentioned her, it wouldn't take more than a few seconds and a good Inter-net search to find her. She had a lively social media presence, and if they couldn't find her there, she'd been pictured in both the print and online version of the newspaper several times. They'd know what she looked like.

BLUE-SUITS MAY KNOW ABOUT YOU. MAY KNOW YOUR FACE IF DANTE TOLD THEM. LAY LOW. TRUST NO ONE.

The spotlight lost them, leaving them dimly illuminated by the cabin's low, green light. He wondered if that helped to pre-serve night vision.

"Get the copters down," said Wheeler, talking to the air again. "Ground transportation only. What's happening at the college?" She cocked her head to the side and cupped her ear. She said to Peter, "Explosion at your high school, and the lights are out on the campus. The explosion has to be a distraction. Is the duffle bag safe? I have men nearby, but there's ... confusion."

Streetlights and houses flowed beneath them. There couldn't be fifty feet between the copter and the tallest trees. Peter imag-ined Christy in the dark cafeteria, Blue-suits pursuing her. No

one to turn to for help. He texted to Christy, WHAT IS HAP-
PENING? Then he made a decision. "Christy Sanders is my
partner. She was in the cafeteria. Can your crew get her out?"

Wheeler covered her ear again. "If they aren't answering,
then assume they're compromised. Go in. You're looking for
Christy Sanders. Get her picture off the high school list."

"Who is not answering?" Peter felt his voice rise. "We need
to go back."

"I told you these were serious people. I've lost contact with
two operatives who were on the cafeteria entrances. That probably means they have been neutralized. I've got more resources
on site, though. This may resolve right now if the Blue-suits
overplayed their hand."

The copter pitched to the side, slowed, and then landed.

When the door opened, Peter jumped out. Green lights,
close to the ground and shrouded, illuminated a large glade
with four other helicopters parked in it and several long tents.
From his phone's GPS, Peter knew they were in BLM property
west of town, north of the interstate. He said to Wheeler, who
unfolded a set of steps to exit the copter, "Wasn't the point of
my leaving was that they would follow me? Leaving was supposed to keep Christy and the duffle bag safe." He checked his
phone. No text from Christy.

"Would this boy, Dante, who was at your house, have told
them about her?"

"Ask him," said Peter, furiously. "Why are you a step behind
in all this?"

Wheeler shrugged. "We would have, but he took off before
he'd been debriefed." She turned her head to the side, a gesture
Peter now recognized to mean she was listening to her agents.
"Divide them into groups. Scrutinize the groups and let them
go. Then, a room by room sweep. Hustle. The army should be
there soon when they realize we took off from the parking lot."

"Here's a puzzler," she said. "One of my men was knocked

out of commission by someone coming into the cafeteria, but the other one was knocked down from behind, from someone coming out. They assume it was a spooked student, but we haven't found Christy yet."

"Maybe they already have the bag. They found Christy and the bag and you aren't looking in the right place." He followed Wheeler as she walked briskly toward a tent.

"If they had the bag, we'd know." Outside the tent, she stopped to face him, her expression a shadowed green in the glade's weird light. "There's a setting on the gun that would end us all if they had it. They'd make a mess of the stability of this reality too. We'd be dead. They'd be gone, and this fine place you call home would disassemble itself."

Wheeler listened to the air again. "Get our people out of there . . . no, don't look for her. Retreat. We'll get it another way." She said to Peter. "The army was faster than we thought. They must have been close by."

"Then let's fly back. I can't do anything here."

"There's plenty *I* can do here, and you can stay safe, where they won't grab you." She pushed the tent flap aside, addressed someone inside, and a large man, about twenty-five with a square jaw and broad shoulders exited.

"Peter, this is Agent Coles. Coles, this is Peter, the boy we've been hunting. We need to keep him out of trouble while he's a guest with us. Could you look after him?"

Coles smiled like it was something he did often, and his handshake was firm and sincere. "Glad to meet you. We've been impressed with how you've managed to stay a step ahead of everyone for so long."

"I didn't know I was being chased most of the time."

"Still, most people wouldn't have lasted. Come on, I can get you some food."

The image of Christy in trouble in the student union filled Peter's head. He left her there! Peter followed behind Cole for a dozen steps before breaking for the woods. The first trees were behind him, and the darkness was nearly complete before Cole called out, "Hey, where'd you go?"

What worried Peter most, ten minutes later, as he tripped over another unseen root, was that the helicopter base wasn't north of the interstate, but south. It wouldn't be the first time the GPS on his phone misled him. If they were south, he'd just be walking deeper and deeper into BLM land, without hope of finding the road or anything else for miles. If they were north of the highway, it couldn't be more than a mile or two, and he should find it pretty soon.

He stopped. Even though it hadn't rained for a day, all the bushes dripped. His pants were soaked to his knees. No message on his phone. He tried calling Christy, but it switched straight to voice mail. The phone almost went back into his pocket before he had a thought and texted his dad that he was okay.

Nothing stirred around him in the black woods, and no sounds reached him other than the steady drip from leaves to ground. He checked his phone to make sure he was still heading in the right direction.

The next step sent him sliding down a short embankment. His knee slammed into a tree trunk that he didn't see, and he spent a few minutes limping heavily until it loosened up, relieving him that it hadn't broken.

A low, windy sound overhead that rustled the trees told him a copter had passed. If they used infrared, he thought, they'd find him instantly. He'd stand out in the cold underbrush like a torch, but the copter didn't pause or change course. The next windy sound he heard was a car passing on the freeway in front of him when he climbed to the top of a short rise.

The second car that came by picked him up. The farmer-boy driver chatted amiably all the way to town about the dangers of hypothermia, pneumonia and bears. "They hunt at night. Most people don't know that," he said.

Peter thanked him when he dropped him off at the gas station near the exit ramp. This would be so much easier if I could drive, thought Peter. As he walked down the street from the gas station, he scanned the yards and porches he passed. This was the less expensive part of town. Lots of vehicles on cinderblocks, beat-up washers and dryers rusting in the backyards, and homes that looked like they only needed to be jacked up and get their wheels remounted to be moved. He spotted what he wanted on the other side of an unpainted picket fence that was falling apart: a bicycle. He checked the address so he could return it later, then quietly lifted the bike over the fence, made sure the tires had pressure, then pedaled away.

It had been about an hour since he'd left the Student Union, which was now in total chaos. Numerous army trucks and police cars were in the parking lot. Policemen were arguing with a preternaturally calm soldier who kept saying in a measured cadence, "No, no, no, no." A television truck arrived, spilling an eager reporter and camera crew. Several searchlights pointed skyward, probing back and forth; students—some of them in pajamas were on the sidewalks—watching what was going on, and everyone had an opinion.

"I heard there was a shooter."

"No, a bomb."

"Police and army, what a waste of taxpayer money."

"Do you think we'll have class tomorrow?"

"I didn't know you had a Buzz Lightyear bathrobe!"

Peter worked his way to the front of the crowd. A line of soldiers held everyone back, fifty yards from the Student Union. "What about the people inside?" Peter asked the nearest soldier.

"I don't know a thing, kid. They're setting up an information table near the admin building."

The cafeteria was lit from the inside with what looked like emergency lighting. Harsh spotlights cast long shadows, and people moved within, but while he watched, the normal lights flickered and then came on, as did the lights in the rest of the building and the dorms behind it.

Peter circled the building to come up from the delivery truck side. Unlike the front, there were no spotlights and only a pair of soldiers more than a hundred feet apart. When they both weren't looking, he sprinted across the delivery platform, then rolled under a loading platform door that hadn't been lowered the whole way. From there, he went through a door into a long hallway that opened onto a balcony above the cafeteria. He hadn't realized the back of the Student Union building was higher than the front. The lights were out and chairs were upside down on the tables, but he could see most of the area below.

Students sat at their tables, talking, many of them angrily. In the room's center, all the jackets, book bags and backpacks were in a pile. Soldiers were examining the coats or emptying the bags brusquely, spilling their contents together. When the bag was empty, the soldier would toss it.

Soldiers who looked more like officers sat at two tables near the front doors. They were interviewing students, and checking IDs. A photographer took a picture of each one. While Peter watched, two of them were allowed to leave. "I need my books!" said one loudly, but the officer shook his head.

Peter sidled along the rail, trying not to step into the light, looking for Christy, thinking, Does the army know what they are looking for? There was a good chance that they were completely clueless. They knew something was going on. They knew about the mystery helicopter brigade, and they knew the spot where Peter torched the tree, but how could they know anything else? This had to be driving them crazy.

He had almost completed his circle of the cafeteria from the second level, when he saw Christy. She was sitting at a table with three college students, chatting. Peter almost called to her in relief, but he stifled the urge. Instead, he took out his phone to text her. No signal. The army must be jamming cell phones.

He felt both relief and helplessness. Christy looked fine, and as long as the other students and soldiers were around, the Blue-suits probably couldn't get her, but the army was searching bags. Where had Christy put the bag? The army might not know what they were looking at when they found it, but they certainly would recognize that it wasn't a normal assortment of college necessities.

And this thought nagged him. Blue-suit had been passing himself off as an FBI agent. Who had authority in a case like this? If the army found the duffle bag, could Blue-suit walk in, flash his FBI credentials, and then confiscate it?

Peter couldn't do anything. He sat in a chair where he could see Christy, but kept himself hidden in shadow. No one knows all the information, he realized. In *The Lord of the Rings*, Frodo was in terrible danger, as was the entire fellowship, but Peter never had the sense that they didn't know what was going on. Orcs were bad. Elves were good (generally), and the beings you met along the way revealed themselves quickly as being on your side or not. Of course, the enemies were confused. The Orcs didn't know exactly what Frodo was carrying, and they quarreled among themselves. Gollum didn't know that Frodo intended on destroying the ring. And Sauron and Wormtongue were just clueless.

Maybe *The Lord of the Rings* wasn't that far off in the way an adventure could go. The best circumstance for the hero was for everyone else to not know all the information.

A shout from below. A bright flash, then glass shattering. Students screamed. Peter jumped to the rail. One of the floor to ceiling windows was knocked out. The soldiers at the doors rushed through the hole. More shouting outside. Another bright flash. Several gunshots. Spotlights on the trucks swiveled, pinning a running man in their crossing beams. He stopped, put his hands up at exactly the same time a soldier, shoulder down, emerged from the darkness, tackling him.

The students had bailed out of their chairs after the gunfire and lay on the floor, covering their heads. Peter ran for the stairs, taking them three at a time. The soldier who had been manning the door at the stair's bottom was gone. Running bent over, Peter jumped over several students, stepped on the back of someone's leg, then skidded to a stop on his belly next to Christy. The soldiers were focused on the busted window. Most of them had gone after whoever blew it up, but the few that remained weren't looking at the students behind them.

"You were gone long enough," she said.

"I've decided the Blue-suits are bad and the fake helicopter army guys are good, at far as we're concerned. There's no way we can let the government or police get the gun. From the sounds of it, at least one of those apps could destroy the entire world."

Christy whispered fiercely, "Why would anyone make an app that would do that? It would kill them too."

"It's something to do with parallel dimensions. This reality could be obliterated, but they wouldn't be here anymore. Total doom to hear Wheeler tell it. Not a bad lady. Very official, though, and business-like. Where's the gun?"

"I'm all right too, thank you for asking," said Christy. "You need more detailed text messages if you don't want someone assuming the worst. 'Don't go home'? What was I supposed to do with that? It's not like I have a secret apartment on this side of town."

Peter opened his mouth, but nothing seemed appropriate. He suggested, lamely, "You could have gone to Village Inn. They're open twenty-four hours."

"I'd have to keep ordering, or they'd throw me out. Besides, do you know who comes into Village Inn late at night? Police officers. I just don't think you had my side of the plan well designed."

"It was an ad lib. I'll do better next time. Also, according to Wheeler, there's only three Blue-suits, including the one in custody. Where's the gun?"

"Behind the fat-free milk in the student commissary, about thirty feet from here. We're okay until they restock."

Peter raised his head. It didn't look like the army managed to hold whoever went through the widow. There was a lot of yelling and soldiers running about outside. One of the trucks roared to life and pulled away.

"We want to get out of here!" a student shouted.

Two boys wearing university baseball team shirts were arguing with each other about walking out. "They're not going to shoot us," said one.

"They shot at someone, doofus. Once gunfire starts, I stay down."

Christy rolled over onto her back. "You know what bums me out most about this is they cut off the cell phones. I'm in a Rock Guitar league. We're supposed to be jamming right now. I play lead. We'll forfeit."

Peter had a realization. Lying on the floor, surrounded by frightened college students, angry soldiers (who recently were shooting), hunted by parallel dimension terrorists and Wheeler's parallel dimension patrol, they were at this moment as safe as they could be. It was unlikely the army would shoot at them, at least as long as they didn't do anything stupid. Whoever went through the window was probably one of the two remaining Blue-suits (who else would have brought explosives to a late-night study session in the Student Union?), and the parallel dimension cops wouldn't expose themselves to the real army.

"If we get the bag," said Peter, "we can go up the stairs to the balcony and out the back door. Once we're clear of the cell phone jamming, I can call Wheeler, and she can have the gun. The whole thing will be behind us, you can teach me how to play the opening chord to "Hard Day's Night" without slicing my fingers open, and I can teach you how to fake a literary essay so well that you won't be faking. All will be well with the world."

Christy looked at him, blonde hair falling across her eyes. "The only thing between us and total happiness is a set of stairs? Let's do it."

Peter started to get up, checked the door, then flopped down, pulling Christy with him. "Blue-suit!" he whispered.

Wearing his FBI jacket, Blue-suit showed a badge to the soldier guarding the entrance. They exchanged words. The soldier returned to his post. Blue-suit strode toward the prostrate students.

"Don't let him see your face," said Peter.

Christy rolled toward him. "Quick, kiss me."

"Tempting. Too obvious. Just cover your head."

The other students, though, were watching Blue-suit with interest. Some were sitting up. Blue-suit scanned the crowd. No one else hid their face.

"FBI, police and army. We can't get any safer," someone said sarcastically. "They should bring in the Marines."

"We're obvious this way too," said Christy.

"Shh! Stay still."

Blue-suit's steps came closer. Peter wanted to scrunch his eyes closed, like when he was a little kid and closing your eyes meant no one could see you.

A hand grabbed him on the shoulder, turned him up, and he was face to face with Blue-suit's tiny, dark eyes and narrow eyebrows. Peter locked stares with him, but Blue-suit showed no recognition. He let go. Christy had rolled to her side. Blue-suit looked at her too before moving on, checking each student, tapping some on the shoulder, as he had with Peter, until he'd seen every student in the cafeteria.

He picked through the pile of empty bags in the center of the room, nodded to the soldier at the door, and exited.

"How is that possible?" said Christy. "He didn't know who

we were. He was in your house! He talked to Dante and your dad. How could he not recognize us?"

Peter laughed in relief. "He *wasn't* the one in our house, at least not the one you put to sleep. He's that guy's twin brother. He must not have the same information his brother had."

They crawled to the commissary's refrigerated display, pulled the bag from behind the milk, then snuck to the door. The students they passed were looking toward the front where the two baseball players argued with the lone soldier at the exit, who now was in charge of keeping a hundred frightened college kids from leaving.

"My dad is a taxpayer, so you work for him," one of the boys yelled.

The door at the bottom of the stairs cut the sound to nothing when it closed behind them.

"There were two soldiers guarding the back when I came in. They might be gone now."

At the loading dock door, Peter got on his hands and knees to check for the guards.

"What made you decide Wheeler should get the bag?" Christy knelt beside him, the bag under her elbows.

"When she met me, she didn't send her men to find you. She didn't threaten me to find out where you were. Instead, she bargained. She had to know you were close by. I think if she was the bad guy, she would have behaved differently."

"I don't see anyone," Christy said. The loading dock appeared to be empty, and both of the building's corners were unguarded. "Am I to understand that your plan was to trust her if she didn't torture you? There's a flaw in your reasoning. It has a torture scenario in it."

Peter squirmed forward, under the gate. "I went on a hunch. I had this epiphany about adventures, and it's that in real life you can't always tell who the good guys and bad guys are."

"I think we're the good guys," she said. They stayed in the

shadow of a delivery truck that was parked in the other bay.

"*We* think we're the good guys. Wheeler probably thinks we're the dumb kids, and she's the good guy; and the Blue-suits probably think that Wheeler is a part of an oppressive government who is restraining their entrepreneurial spirit, while you and I are pesky annoyances. Oh, and the Blue-suits may believe our dimension is disposable, which would be what you would think if there were an infinite number of dimensions to sort through."

Christy looked both ways, then sprinted for the sidewalk and line of trees on the other side of the street. Peter followed, feeling horribly exposed in the open, and only slightly better as they trotted down the grass-covered hill toward classrooms and dorms.

Peter said, "We need to resolve this and get home. My dad's probably going crazy, and your parents will be worried too."

"I called them earlier." They hit a sidewalk intersection, turned so they were no longer running directly away from the Student Union, and slowed to a walk. "Told them I'd be out late."

"Do you think they'll buy that? There were cops and fake army guys at my house not too long ago. There was an explosion at the high school and sirens all over town. They'll at least want to know you are safe."

"What my mom would be more concerned about is that I'm running around on a freezing September night without a coat. I wonder if the gun has a bubble-of-warmth app. That would be useful." She held up the bag.

"Do you want to try a random app? You could fry our brain cells. You could turn living things inside out. Wheeler didn't make it sound like any of the options include rainbows and unicorns. Let's get inside. I can call Wheeler when we're out of the cold."

The dorms were locked, though, with card-swipe readers.

No one answered when Peter pushed the entrance bell button, even though he could hear it ringing inside. The entire school was probably on lock-down. Every building could be inaccessible, but the Grayson Plant Studies building, an imposing, multi-story edifice, was open. They stepped into the foyer, a huge room, forty yards across and three stories tall, filled with palm trees, vines, and ferns. Water trickled and fell down rock faces on both sides of the door.

"Wow," said Christy. "I want to go to this school when I graduate. They know how to do a major the right way. We have to find the music classrooms!"

Peter walked deeper into the room. A vine enshrouded desk with sliding glass windows was marked RECEPTION AND REGISTRATION. The sign above the darkened hallway to the left read BIOFORMS A, and the one to the desk's right was BIOFORMS B. Display cases, many lit by purple grow lights, lined the walls. It smelled like a rain forest.

Christy said, "What's that on your shoulder?"

Peter reached around, detached a white button off his back, but barely saw it before a familiar voice said, "That would be a tracer, young lady." Blue-suit stood in the exit behind them, still in his FBI jacket, with a gun in his hand: an ordinary, black gun like a police officer might carry. "I couldn't very well do anything with the army all around. Besides, you didn't have the bag. Would you drop it, please?"

The question had no hint of a request in it.

The bag hit the floor.

"Step back."

Peter glanced up, to the left and right. Blue-suit couldn't get the bag. If he did, everything ended. He'd zap them—who knew with what—then rift himself anywhere he'd want to go. Peter had worked out the possibilities. If people from Wheeler's world could jump universes, they'd be uncatchable. How hard was it to make a jump? What kind of equipment was needed?

If it was small enough to be on Blue-suit, like a watch or a belt, he'd jump from here. If it took more equipment, then he'd need to go somewhere, but he'd jump just the same. Peter wondered if a shift from one world to another took calculations. Was it easy or hard?

None of that mattered now, though. He and Christy were expendable. In movies, the hero always figured out what to do at this point. He'd have a button to push, or a hidden weapon, or a backup plan that would kick in. But he and Christy were in the middle of a bare floor, thirty feet from anything. They couldn't run. He didn't have a secreted weapon. He couldn't charge Blue-suit and take the gun from him.

The dark-eyed man, keeping the gun aimed, knelt at the bag. "Putting everyone to sleep at the house was elegant. We have an easy counter to that effect. The sleep trick won't work again, but I have to admit the efficiency of it." He opened the bag. This would be where a flash-bang exploded, stunning him, but that didn't happen either.

Blue-suit paused, reached in, and brought out a book. It looked like the same Econ text the cashier had been reading when Peter bought the hot chocolates, what seemed like hours ago. Another book came out and another. Blue-suit dumped the bag, scattering two more books.

"That's ingenious," he said. "Where's my property?"

Neither of them spoke, but Peter thought about the next step. He'd threaten to hurt one or the other until the one who knew gave him the information. Peter hoped that when Blue-suit shot him in the leg, or knocked in his teeth, that he wouldn't immediately say that Christy had hidden the gun.

But a fifty-fifty chance said that Blue-suit would hurt Christy first. The only way to delay Blue-suit would be to lie. If he could get him to take them somewhere, if he could get him to look away long enough, he could call for help.

"I hid it," said Peter. His voice quivered.

"Glad to hear it. We don't need her." Blue-suit swung the gun around to point at Christy.

"He's lying," said Christy, her voice as calm as answering a question in class. Before Blue-suit could react, she said, "Or I'm lying. I'll tell you this truth, though. Only one of us knows where the contents of your bag are. You can't kill either one without risking losing it all."

"Also ingenious," he said. "I don't have to kill either of you. Here's how it's going to go. I'm going to break your fingers, little girl, one at a time until the two of you agree on the same story." He pointed the gun at Peter. "Sit. If you try to get up, I'll blow your kneecap off, and then I'll shoot hers too for good measure."

Peter sat. Blue-suit moved toward Christy. "You know, you two have been a terrible aggravation. I think when I'm done here, I'm going to visit as many of the nearby worlds as I can, the ones closest to this one, and kill you both in each."

The entrance door pushed open a couple of inches. Peter caught the motion and saw the sputtering ball rolling through, towards them. Blue-suit turned at the noise.

The explosion deafened Peter, even though he'd got his hands over his ears in time. Blue-suit had lost the gun, but he wasn't looking for it. He vanished down **BIOFORMS B** hallway at a full sprint. Peter helped a stunned Christy to her feet.

Dante held the door open gesturing at them, his mouth moving, but Peter could barely hear over the ringing.

The three ran from the Grayson Plant Studies building like gazelles, in the opposite direction that Blue-suit had fled, passing dorm after classroom building after dorm, until they reached the edge of campus.

They hid beneath a foot bridge that crossed a stream dividing the school grounds from the last greenway before a bordering street. A suburban neighborhood, cars neatly parked on driveways, porch lights on, looked peaceful, inviting, and so out of touch with what Peter had been experiencing that the scene had a surreal feel to it, like a painting where the colors were a shade too bright, and the images too idealized to be of this world.

A streetlight reflected off the stream's surface, lighting them as they caught their breath. Christy pressed her hands against her ears, released, and did it again. "Am I bleeding?" she asked loudly, "from my ears?"

"Cherry bomb?" said Peter. Most of the ringing had faded, but his ears hurt.

Dante grinned. "You never know when you'll need one," he said. He held up his phone. "I've been tracking you since the cops left your house. You've made some strange-ass moves. Were you in an airplane at one point? Worried me when the signal vanished at the college." He turned to Christy. "You put us to sleep! I was dizzy for an hour after."

Peter said, "What happened, Dante? Why were you and Blue-suit at my house?"

A car drove down the street in front of them. They moved deeper under the bridge and farther out of sight.

Dante's face became tragic. "I'm so, so sorry, Peter. I thought that Blue-suit really was FBI, that you were right about getting rid of the gun, so I called him and told him I could lead him to it. I knew I was wrong as soon as we got to your house. He shouldn't get the gun, Peter. I was crazy to trust him." He hung his head down between his knees, then he snapped upright. "How the hell did he get away from the police? Your dad said he was going to press charges. The last time I saw Blue-suit, he was in handcuffs. The cops were talking false imprisonment or kidnapping charges."

"Oh, that wasn't him. I mean the one you took to the house. He's a twin. He has a brother. I thought they were clones, but there's just two of them that look alike." Peter faced Christy. "How'd a bunch of books end up in the bag? Where's the gun?"

"It's still in the cafeteria. You were gone a long time, Peter, so I was thinking that if they saw the bag, they'd go for that. They might even have grabbed the bag, run off and not realized that they didn't have what they wanted until they were long gone. I'd made the switch an hour before you showed up. That plan almost backfired, though. I was afraid Blue-suit wasn't going to look in the bag before shooting us. I was about to tell him he'd better check but he did without prompting."

"That's crazy. When we left the cafeteria, you thought we were going to give the bag to Wheeler. Why would you take a fake bag?"

"Maybe I don't trust Wheeler as much as you do. Her reaction to getting the bag could tell us a lot. At least that's what I was thinking when you said we were going to give it to her. Not handing her the real deal the first time through seemed like a good idea. If she's Blue-suit's enemy, though, I think I like her."

Peter looked at them in wonderment. "Well, you're both crafty. Blue-suits didn't know what they were getting into when they tangled with us. I think we ought to tell each other what we're doing from now on though. Agreed?"

Dante and Christy nodded.

"I've found out a lot about the gun. Wheeler . . ." he looked at Dante, ". . .she's the commander of the fake army helicopter guys . . . told me that it can destroy everything. If Blue-suit gets it, the Earth is done, and it's too powerful to give to anyone on Earth. We have to give it to her. She'll take it wherever she came from, and then close the door so no one from their world can come back here. At least, that's the deal I'm going to propose if you guys agree. I can call her. End this thing right now."

"Go ahead," said Dante.

Christy said, "Don't we . . . sort of . . . have to have the gun if we call her? We've got all the same problems still. She can't go get the gun because the army is all over the Student Union building, and if we wait too long, someone else is going to find it just like we did and start trying apps. They might not be as lucky as we were. We could end up with a Blue-suit of our own making."

"Dang," said Peter. He leaned back against the cold brick of the bridge's underside and closed his eyes. He'd never felt so tired.

"How are we going to do it?" asked Dante.

"I don't know. Peter?"

Peter took a deep breath, sat up, and took control. "Here's what we'll do: Christy and I are going back to the Student Union. We should be able to get in the same way we got out. We could be lucky and the soldiers could have already gone home. They have to think that whoever went through the window and got away was their mystery. The only reason they came to the campus in the first place is they traced the helicopter there. Once they clear all the students, the case will move in a different direction for them. They think it's all about the helicopters. Christy and I will go in to get the stuff she dumped from the bag. Dante, you need to be our invisible cover. Blue-suit doesn't know that you're helping, so if you see things are going badly, you can swoop in. You have more cherry bombs?"

Dante dug into his pocket and brought out two. "It surprised him once. Do you think it will work twice?"

Peter's ears still pulsed with the first explosion. "That's the loudest sound I've ever heard. I don't believe being prepared will make a difference. If nothing else, it will attract a lot of attention."

On the way back to the Student Union, they had to go the long way around The Grayson Botanical Science classrooms. Two police cars, their lights flashing, were parked out front. "See," said Peter, "I told you they'd attract attention. The bummer is that unless Blue-suit went back, the cops are going to find a gun in the foyer. They might decide they have to do a building to building search for the shooter. Too much has gone on here tonight for it to be swept under the rug."

As they watched, another police car raced toward the class-room building. Students had come out of the dorms, coats wrapped around themselves to see what was going on. Others were on their balconies.

A megaphone voice from one of the police cars announced, "This campus is still under lockdown. Students should return to their dorms and stay clear of the windows until we are sure that everyone is secure."

None of the students moved. There were a chorus of boos from the students on the balconies.

"You kids need to get inside," the megaphone announced, sounding more peeved this time.

"It's impossible to do a lockdown on a Friday night," said Christy. "The parties are in full swing. College students will turn this into a drinking game."

"That may be to our advantage," said Peter. Proving his point, a loud group of students, most of them holding beer bottles or plastic cups, passed them going the other way. A round-faced guy, a six pack in one hand and a reading light, its electric cord dragging on the cement in the other, saw Christy, and said, "Look at her! She's gotta be freezin' to deaf." He dropped the six pack, breaking a bottle, and then carefully put the reading lamp down before stripping off his coat. "Can't haf a lady freezin' to def."

Dante said, "Waste of a good beer."

Christy shrugged her shoulders and took the coat. "I *am* freezing!" she said as the drunken group left.

They trudged up the grassy hill toward the Student Union. "Dante, this is where we split up. The police may have moved their attention to the botany building, and we can get the gun."

Dante ran to get to the building's front.

Peter couldn't tell if the army still occupied the parking lot. He checked his phone to see where Dante had placed himself. No signal. The jamming wasn't lifted yet. There were no guards in back, which he took as a good sign.

From the rail overlooking the cafeteria, the place was a mess. Backpacks, books, notebooks, water bottles and a host of other student staples were in a loose pile in the middle. Tables and chairs had been pushed aside for the search. The janitors will hate this, Peter thought. One military truck remained in the parking lot, but the soldiers were not leaving. Three of them gathered around a table, and it looked like they were setting up a listening station as they had near Peter's house. They must figure if a stealth helicopter landed here once, it might come again.

"No one's around," whispered Christy.

"That jacket smells. What is that?"

She brought the sleeve up to her face. "Pot, I think. Lamp boy hangs out with a decadent crowd. Don't care. It's warm."

They went down the stairs, stepping softly.

Without people in it, the cafeteria felt cavernous. Three quarters of the lights were out—the room must have switched into an energy-saving mode—so the periodic bright spots stood as islands of light in a sea of shadows.

"I'll get a bag." Peter stayed low as he slunk to the room's middle, sure that anyone looking in from the parking lot would see him. He grabbed an empty canvas backpack with an EAT VEGAN patch on the front, then backed up, hoping no one was paying attention to the cafeteria anymore. He wondered where Dante was, and if he could see them.

Except for the lights in the refrigerated displays, the commissary was completely dark. Christy, on her hands and knees, unloaded several quarts of milk from the dairy case, setting the gun and the plexiglass bricks to the side. Peter used the bricks to line the bottom of the bag before putting the gun on top.

Peter zipped the bag shut and slipped a strap over his shoulder. "Out the back door. Get away from the jamming signal. Call Wheeler for a copter ride, and then we're done. We could be home by midnight."

"I won't miss it," said Christy. "I don't want to know what the other icons do. We don't need this kind of technology."

Peter started toward the stairs with Christy behind him.

"Then you won't mind giving it up," said a voice, followed by an electrical sounding jolt.

Christy lay face down on the floor, an arm extended uncomfortably above her head. Blue-suit stood over her, a black device the size of a deck of cards in his hand.

"Don't move," Blue-suit said. "Don't think about doing anything at all. The girl's unconscious, but I have other settings. A twist of a button, and she's dead." He kicked her in the back to demonstrate, which elicited from Christy a low moan. "See. Not dead."

Blue-suit shifted his gaze from one side to the other. "Where's your bomb-throwing friend? I should have taken care of him while he was sleeping at your house. Guess we didn't convince him which side he should be on."

Peter held himself still, afraid that if he moved Blue-suit would zap Christy again. Dante has to be outside, somewhere, Peter thought, or he could be on the balcony overhead, but he wouldn't be in position to do anything, and now the plan to use a second cherry bomb seemed stupid. If Dante threw it, the remaining soldiers outside would be on them instantly, and, as far as they knew, Blue-suit was FBI. He could walk right through them with the bag and the gun and no challenge.

He should have guessed, thought Peter. Of course Blue-suit would be able to figure out where Christy had left the gun. The cafeteria was where they'd met. He'd been waiting for them to leave so he could catch them. No gun? Blue-suit just needed to wait for them to come back to the cafeteria and show him where it was. Peter wished he'd called Wheeler before moving back into the no-cell zone. That way the cavalry could be on the way, if she was willing to draw attention to her copters again.

Christy rolled over with a groan. Blue-suit stepped to the side, but kept the weapon poised. "Bring me the bag."

Peter picked it up. He experienced a vivid sense of deja-vu. They were playing the Grayson Botanical Sciences building confrontation again. The stakes were the same.

He'd read thrillers and adventure novels. He'd seen a zillion movies and played video games. What would James Bond do in this situation or Laura Croft or Indiana Jones or Doc Savage? He couldn't let Blue-suit get the bag, but none of the options worked. He could run, but Blue-suit would kill Christy. Or, as an FBI agent, Blue-suit could have the soldiers stop him in the parking lot.

Peter didn't know martial arts. He didn't have a hidden knife, or even a ballpoint pen. Those who don't learn from the past are bound to repeat it, he thought. He didn't have a weapon on him last time either. He should have asked the drunk college kids if any of them had a knife. Blue-suit won. Peter had to give him the gun.

But he couldn't cause the world's death.

Desperate times, he thought, call for stupid maneuvers.

He held out the backpack. Blue-suit, grinning grimly, reached for it.

Peter dropped the bag an inch short, then threw all his weight into Blue-suit's chest as he reflexively bent to catch it.

Even as they careened across the room, Peter thought this would end in a hurry.

All Peter knew of real fighting—not the pretend fighting in the movies where everyone moved too competently and too fast—was what he'd seen in fights at school. They ended the same way, with the combatants wrestling. He and Dante theorized that what really happened in a fight, even if the boys were tough, macho warriors of the hallways, was that they really were afraid of getting hit. So after a showy punch or two, almost always an artless roundhouse swing that anyone could see coming from a mile away, the two would grapple. It was much harder to be hit in a clinch than if you were standing at slugging distance.

The only real fist fight he'd seen in the school, and it wasn't much of a fight, was between two girls. Many of the girl fights he'd seen *started* with wrestling (and hair pulling and clothes tearing). There were no punches, expect for the one time a thick-shouldered girl who played rugby got into it with a slender band girl, who didn't look any bulkier than her flute, over the rugby player's boyfriend. She claimed the flute player had been flirting with him. The flute player said, "Nope," and put down her books. When the rugby player charged, probably intending on squashing the other girl with her momentum, the flute player gracefully stepped to one side, and threw one short punch that caught the other girl on the side of her face. The rugby player hit the tiles, screaming about her ear, while the flute player picked up her books like nothing had happened, and went to class.

Peter wished he was as graceful as that flute player. Blue-suit grunted. Tried to swing his shocker around, but Peter's charge continued to drive him backwards, until a chair caught the back of Blue-suit's knees, and they went down.

Somehow, Peter ended up on the heavier man's back, his arm around Blue-suit's throat and his legs wrapped around his waist.

A cherry bomb exploded ten feet inside the broken window, still amazingly loud in the enclosed space, but it didn't bother Blue-suit at all, who also didn't seem hindered by the choke hold, and was prying Peter's leg grip loose.

A drowning person is supposed to see his life flash by in the last instant. When someone is stopped at a red light, and the sound of screeching tires makes him look up in the rear-view mirror to see a truck skidding toward him, time slows. For Peter, time slowed. The cherry bomb's smoke eddied like a sinuous ghost toward the ceiling. Christy had sat up and was pulling the gun from the bag. Peter thought, the sleep-ray won't work! Blue-suit inexorably leveraged Peter's locked legs off of him, and as slow as time had seemed to be going, no time at all passed before Blue-suit was kneeling on Peter's chest, forcing the air from his lungs.

"Soldiers are coming," yelled Christy.

Blue-suit looked behind him where the first man was coming through the broken window. He swore, pushed off Peter's chest, and ran for the bag, knocking Christy aside while grabbing the gun from her hands and scooping the backpack off the ground. He ran for the door to the stairs.

Peter tried to get up. He had to stop him. He could hit him with a chair. Anything before Blue-suit could have time to use the gun. Once Blue-suit picked the right icon—and who knew what most of the gun's functions were—he would win.

But something ground in Peter's chest, and he had a hard time getting a full breath.

"Stop him," he gasped.

"It's all right," Christy said, inexplicably.

Blue-suit made it to the door. The soldiers weren't even looking at him, and Peter couldn't take a deep enough breath to call.

Christy said again, "It's all right."

The door opened. A horrible orange light spilled out. Peter's ears popped as papers were swept off the floor toward the orange glow. In front of Blue-suit, whose dark shape partly eclipsed the scene, the orange world's long, rolling landscape reflected its horrible sun. Peter couldn't see the hill's top through the door, but he knew the malevolent creature waited there, maybe looking toward them this time. Peter wanted to close his eyes, but he watched instead. Cups and loose papers slid on the floor toward the opening. Blue-suit grabbed for the door frame, held on, fighting the wind. For a second, he dangled, his feet off the ground, then he tried to shift his grip, slipped and was sucked away. He screamed, but the sound came from a distance, and when the rift in the stairwell winked closed, the scream snapped off as if it had never been.

Papers settled.

Blue-suit, the bag and gun were gone.

34

Wheeler's medic wrapped a compression bandage around Peter's chest and gave him a pill he said was a muscle relaxant. "You'll want to talk to your own doctor tomorrow, but I think it's just a cracked rib. You're lucky he didn't put more pressure on it."

Standing to the side, in Wheeler's command tent, Christy looked on. "See," she said, "if he worked out, he'd have muscle to protect his skeletal structure. He needs to pump iron."

The medical area was at the tent's far end. Dark canvas formed the wall behind the medic's partners. Wheeler stood on the other side. Behind her, tables filled with electronic equipment were lit by lights hanging from the long pole that formed the tent's peak. Soldiers sat at most of the tables, reading screens while spouting indecipherable jargon to each other, like, "We have LOSA on the UFT, locked and charted."

Finally, Peter felt he could take a deep breath. From the time that Wheeler's crew rushed in to pick him up, and during the long ride in a shiny black SUV with heavily tinted windows, until the medic had done his magic, Peter had been breathing in short, painful hitches. His head swam, and he was petrified that the next breath he wouldn't be able to get enough air. Once Wheeler decided that Peter probably wasn't going to die, she'd spent the ride talking earnestly to Christy.

Peter swung his legs off the bed. He sat unsteadily. "You cut my shirt off. What am I supposed to wear?" The medic dug into a cabinet next to one filled with boxes and bottles. He tossed Peter a shirt that looked exactly like the one he was wearing, complete with CARTER on an embroidered patch above the pocket. It didn't fit badly. "I thought you guys only had helicopters," Peter said to Wheeler. "Where'd the cars come from?"

"Your army was listening for the copters. We opened the rift to bring in a couple of less conspicuous forms of transportation. Dante texted us when he saw what was going on in the cafeteria."

Christy said, "He must have run like a quarter of a mile to get out from under the jamming too. Tough choice for him, I'll bet, toss a cherry bomb, call the cops, or come in and help."

"What happened in there? How did Blue-suit . . . disappear?" He shivered, thinking about Blue-suit flying into the orange world.

Wheeler nodded toward Christy. "She set a trap."

Christy closed her eyes. "I knew I could open the portal behind the door, but couldn't he rift his way out once he got there? I mean, if the Cyclops-dogs didn't get him first, or that . . . being on the hill?"

"'Cyclops-dogs? Good name for them. That's one of the few worlds we know that you can rift into with such a small device, and he couldn't rift out. It's not a human-friendly place. The air's wrong for us, for one, and if that didn't render him unconscious within seconds, there's the . . . what did you call it? . . . 'being' on the hill. If you look at it, I mean really see it, it burns out your brain. He's gone. We claimed the first brother from the police. Christy flushed the second brother into orange world, and their partner rifted away without what they came for. I know that sounds unlikely, but it's true. You are back to normal."

"You can't say anything 'unlikely,' as far as I'm concerned. We've been living in unlikely for a week," said Peter.

"According to Christy," said Wheeler, smiling for the first

time Peter could remember, "we're done here. Through your efforts, the largest threat to our world and yours went through that rift and it can't get back. The technology in the bag can't be duplicated if the bag is gone."

"That's incredible, that one gun could be so dangerous. If didn't even look that well-made." Peter buttoned the borrowed shirt. He couldn't feel the grinding in his chest at all, and he felt unusually content. He wondered if that was the muscle relaxant. He thought about asking if Carter wouldn't give him a couple more to take home, just in case.

"Yes," said Wheeler. She checked a tablet a soldier gave her, checked an item, then gave it back. "The gun, as bad as it was, though, wasn't the worst danger. It was the component motherboards. He had dozens of them. Properly assembled, not crudely, like his gun, the people using them would have been unstoppable."

"What?" Peter asked. "You mean those bricks?" He thought about the first time he'd picked one up, and it felt like it buzzed.

"One of those 'bricks' is the heart of his gun. The gun is just a tiny power source, like a flashlight battery, and a trigger to activate the component. The bricks are what this is all about. The two brothers and their friends would use, sell or distribute them as they saw fit. Our only hope was to stop the plan before they had a chance to split the bricks up. We almost had them in our world. They were on the run, so they dumped the bag in a trash bin, planning on coming back later, but the trash was rifted out before they returned, which is how it ended up here."

Peter wrinkled his brow. "Our little dump is a part of an inter-dimensional sanitation system?"

Wheeler laughed. She seemed to genuinely be in a good mood now. Peter thought she came across much less grim in this happier frame of mind. "It was an accidental one. A really big shipment through a rift can have 'spillage.' We can track the spillage. Your 'dump' was the result of pushing too much through at the same time with out-of-tune commercial equipment. I like to think about how they felt when they went to retrieve the bag and everything had been rifted away."

In the background, soldiers were moving equipment from the tent. They folded tables and stacked chairs.

Wheeler led them outside to the SUV.

Peter said, "You know, an all-black SUV with tinted windows as part of a conspiracy involving inter-dimensional smuggling and world-ending technology is a bit of a cliché. You could have gone with something original, like a station wagon."

She gave him a quizzical look. "One of my men will drive you home." She put her hands behind her back. "You're welcome to tell anyone you want about what's happened this week. It won't matter to us, but there isn't much chance you'll be believed."

Peter shook his head. "Probably not."

Christy said, "This world jumping trick you guys have, it's something you invented?"

"Surprising, isn't it," said Wheeler. "We've had the technology for years. At first it required a huge amount of equipment and energy. Only wealthy firms or governments could afford to use the technique, and we didn't know the possibilities in the beginning, but things get smaller and cheaper. A person-sized rift unit could fit in a suitcase. That's the way our world went. You have fans without propellers. A Dyson fan? We don't have that. No cell phones either. Worlds advance along different lines. That's how the 'gun' came about, combined technologies from different worlds using different approaches to solving problems; all possible in your world. Nothing that defies physics. They just haven't been done here yet. I've been to a place where they discovered space travel, but they're doing it in wooden spaceships. Almost no metals in their dimension."

Wheeler shook each of their hands. "It has been an education, working with you. Thank you again for your help."

"We won't be able to talk to you again, will we?" said Peter. The prospect saddened him some. He'd read that science fiction's appeal was in its "sense of wonder." It was a literature that reminded readers, even if it was just in their imagination, that the universe contained infinite possibilities, that surprise and awe were still possible, even when existence seemed boring and mundane. He didn't think that he'd forget the events of this week, but they would only exist in his memory. Memories fade. He almost couldn't picture his mother's face anymore. Memory slowly absorbed her, burnished away her edges, made her hard to see. Today the universe opened for Peter, like a brilliant flower. Tomorrow the memory would start to lose its shape. Today he saw the tent and helicopters; he could touch them. Today he heard Wheeler's voice and saw the wrinkles at the corners of her eyes. Tomorrow . . . well, tomorrows erase todays.

"No. We won't come back. You don't have the means to reach us." She touched her forehead, as if tipping her cap, and opened the SUV door for them.

Wheeler said, "What will you tell your parents?"

No lies came to mind. Peter thought that he might just try to tell his dad exactly what happened. After all, Dad had been sleep-rayed, he'd seen Blue-suit and knew that he'd wanted something of Peter's. In fact, his dad was the next closest human being to know what had been happening. The school and army would never know who the fake FBI guy was, assuming they ever discovered he was fake. The army would never find out who piloted the very quiet helicopters that they'd been hunting for several days. The destruction in the dump glade would remain a mystery forever. Peter's dad, at least, deserved a chance to know the truth. And who could tell, Peter thought, Dad is cool. He might believe me. Christy and Dante would have a tougher time talking to their parents than he would.

"Did you already take Dante home?" he asked.

Wheeler looked down. "We couldn't find him. We're hoping

that he is on his way now. I have an agent watching his house to let us know when he gets there. I didn't want to alarm you, but we have good equipment for picking up rift signatures. From our readings, it looks like two people went through. We don't know who the extra person was."

"It couldn't be Dante," said Peter. "Why would he go with him?"

"We don't know that it was Dante," said Wheeler. "It's just that he's not home yet, and he was near where the third man was when he jumped from this world. If Dante tried to capture him or to stop him from fleeing, he could have been caught in the rift field. Somebody extra went through."

"Then you need to follow him," said Christy. She stood beside Peter, holding his elbow hard. "We have to get him back."

Wheeler shook her head. "There's no way to tell where they went in all the infinite choices. We couldn't land where they landed no matter how often we tried unless we knew the settings on their machine. The rift is a perfect hideout."

On the ride home, Peter and Christy didn't talk. Peter's thoughts ran on a twinned track. In one version, Dante was walking into his house, triumphant after the long night. They had won! The gun was safe and the two Blue-suits and their partner were gone. In the other track, though, Peter pictured Dante outside the Student Union in the darkened parking lot. He's thrown his cherry bomb. Soldiers rush the building. A bright, orange light appears at the back of the cafeteria where the first Blue-suit would disappear. Then, Dante sees a man who is also studying the scene. He's not a policeman, soldier or college student. Maybe he's someone that Dante and Peter had seen at school in the last week, hanging around. He was Blue-suit's silent partner. Maybe Dante recognized him. The man standing in the parking lot opens a suitcase or a small chest . . . Wheeler said that the rifting equipment was bigger than the gun . . . and he starts to adjust controls within it, or maybe it has a hologram screen that pops into existence, like the gun, and Dante recognizes it for what it was. He rushes forward.

What did he hope to accomplish?

Peter thought, it doesn't matter what Dante had in mind, he always rushes forward. That is his style.

35

Dante didn't come home. The police interviewed Peter, Christy, and most of the sophomore class over the next week at school. Principal Rappe and the teachers tried to cooperate, but between the events of the previous week and this new round of interruptions, they clearly wanted to get back to an unexciting school year.

He did see Wheeler again, at the end of the week. She stood on the street corner next to the school, still in her long raincoat. The weather had grown steadily colder since the weekend. Wind blew steadily. Snow was expected by Sunday.

"You didn't find him," said Peter.

Wheeler shook her head. "I wouldn't give up hope. We don't know where he went, but the people who took him know where they came from. They know this location. There's a chance Dante can find his way back if he can get the coordinates. The man he went with doesn't have a record of hurting people. There's no reason to think he'd hurt your friend."

"Aren't they all bad?" Peter felt miserable. He hadn't worn a thick enough jacket either. The wind cut through it, chilling him hard.

"No, Peter, I don't think so. Some are in it to make money. Some want power. Some, though, are zealots. They see themselves as pioneers. They're rift riders, gathering what they can to advance humanity."

Peter tried to picture the Blue-suits as heroes, but what he saw instead was the tree exploding into flame, and how the flame looked like the edges of the rift world they'd found at the ball field. He remembered the threats. Nothing sounded good about that.

Wheeler shoved her hands deeper into her coat pockets and turned away from the wind. "It's a mistake to paint any group of people with the same brush. They're dangerous, seriously dangerous. We thought they were exploring too deeply, without safeguards. They needed to be stopped, and we stopped them with your help, but they wouldn't necessarily kill Dante. They might even just send him back."

Peter nodded, but his heart ached. Dante was gone.

36

Normally Peter took the bus home from school or rode his bike, but today seemed like a good day to walk. The prediction of snow on Sunday was a bust. By 1:00 on Monday, the temperature had climbed to sixty degrees. The last talk with Wheeler was just a part of the oddities. Despite the weekend passing, strangers still disrupted the school. Since one of the school's dumpsters beside the building had exploded, leaving a circle of blackened brick and several broken windows, government agents kept going in and out of the building. It turned out that the ATF investigated explosions in government buildings, so the police, FBI (real ones, probably) and other official types walked through the halls all day. Crime scene tape marked off half of the student parking lot, but the students adapted easily since the practice field still had tape cordoning off part of it while the military finished their investigation in Melville Park.

For the first time in his academic career, Peter failed to turn in homework. Mrs. Pickerel collected the final drafts of the *Of Mice and Men* essays. Peter had forgotten to do his. He'd spent Saturday explaining and re-explaining to his dad the events of the past week. Dad said, "I'll take this story under advisement," but he didn't say whether he believed him. Midway through the first rendition, Peter thought it was possible that Dad would want to check him for drug use the next time he had a physical.

Sunday, Peter stayed in his room. He slept in then spent the day with the curtains drawn to keep it dark, streaming black and white movies: *Them*, *The Incredible Shrinking Man*, *The Thing*, *Abbot and Costello Meet the Invisible Man* and *Donovan's Brain*. He was trying not to think much. He certainly didn't consider doing homework.

Impossibly, Christy had finished her paper.

The return of Vice Principal Bovine hardly sparked a comment. A home break-in didn't measure up to the rest of the week.

Most of last week's clouds had cleared. The sun shone with that bright November light that showed every autumn leaf while reminding him that summer once had warmed this spot. It's Indian summer, Peter thought.

A mile of his walk home was on a narrow, gravel-shouldered two-lane strip of asphalt where the houses were a hundred yards back and the driveways were dirt. The bus he'd normally ride rumbled up the road behind him, so he stepped another couple yards off the shoulder to let it pass. On this part of the route, it stopped every couple of driveways to let students off. It pulled over just beyond him, red lights flashing. Two boys, six years old or so, jumped off, talking animatedly. They both carried baseball mitts and wore Pirates Little League shirts. The baseball season had ended in September, but he remembered how he and Dante wore their uniforms until Christmas, how they had played catch even when it snowed. He wondered what positions the two boys played. Were they infielders? Had they ever turned a double play that ended the game to win them a trophy? Were they best friends?

Christy got off the bus after them and waited on the shoulder for him to walk to her. She turned toward home. They walked without speaking. Finally, she said, "I tried playing the guitar on Sunday. Dad bought me a Johnny Winter slide. He said it was the 'Cadillac of guitar slides,' but it was too long. I couldn't control it. I thought I should go old-school and use a coke bottle neck instead."

Peter wasn't sure exactly what she was talking about, but he said, "Uh huh," as if he did. He didn't feel much like conversation.

He kicked a rock the size and shape of a plum. It skittered to a stop ten feet away, and when they got to it, Christy kicked it another ten feet. Peter's third kick went sideways into the weeds off the shoulder. He was sorry the game stopped.

Christy continued, as if there'd been no pause. "I just didn't have a guitar lick in me anyways. I watched movies instead."

Peter perked up. "Really? Which ones?"

"Whenever the Poms get together for a movie night, they want whatever's come out last. I keep suggesting old films. Did you ever see *Casablanca*? Ingrid Bergman's in it. She's amazing. She won an Oscar for *Gaslight*, which wasn't nearly as good. But I think I just like black and white movies. They aren't about computer graphics."

"What about *King Kong*, the Fay Wray version? That's fantastic claymation. No electronic trickery there."

"Exactly what I mean," she said. "Have you seen *The Incredible Shrinking Man*? It's one of my favorites."

They talked about films for the rest of the walk, and when they got home they stood on the lawn between their houses debating the finer points of Audie Murphy versus Glen Ford's westerns.

Finally, Christy's mom poked her head out her front door to call Christy in for dinner.

"I'll see you tomorrow," she said.

"Sounds good."

But at midnight, while Peter worked on the late *Of Mice and Men* paper, she texted him, and they exchanged texts back and forth until 2:00 am, when the paper was done.

37

A week later, the crime scene tape was gone. The black smudge on the high school where the bomb had exploded had been cleaned and the broken windows replaced.

The army left Melville Park. The official explanation was that a "micro-burst," an incredibly powerful and very localized storm had damaged trees and caused the destruction. Their press release called it a "one in a billion phenomenon."

After the incidents at the college, security was tightened. The board of regents briefly discussed putting metal detectors on the doors into the Student Union, but the gun rights advocates, who'd been lobbying for conceal and carry rights on campus, argued against such an anti-second amendment maneuver.

For Peter, though, the news that caught his eye was a thirty-second interview with a farmer north of town who claimed a chupacabra had cleaned out his chickens. The reporter suggested that chupacabras were supposed to live in Latin America, and that they were mythical creatures anyways. The farmer said, "If you'd seen what I'd seen, you wouldn't be calling it mythical. Its head was all bone and teeth, and I'll never forget that one eye staring at me while it ate my prize-winning Wyandotte. Best chicken I ever owned."

*

"You two are thick as thieves," Peter's dad said at dinner. "So, is she your girlfriend or what?"

Peter poured gravy over the Thanksgiving dressing. Most of the time, he and Dad foraged for meals. They'd shop on Sunday, grabbing whatever looked good, and then ate when the mood struck them. A sit-down dinner wasn't their habit, but on Thanksgiving Dad had always done the cooking for the family, finding the biggest turkey that would fit in their oven so they could live off the leftovers for weeks. The meal itself was a production. Dad put down a tablecloth, brought out the good china and silverware, lit candles, poured sparkling apple cider, and carved the turkey with surgical precision. "Your mom always liked Thanksgiving," he'd said earlier in the meal.

"No, we're friends."

Dad spooned out a second helping of mashed potatoes. "That's the best way to do it," he said enigmatically. "I got your e-mail with all those guitar links. Are you doing some pre-Christmas hinting?"

"You said you never know what to get me. A little amplifier would be nice too."

"Are you going to blast the house with distortion and reverb?"

"Do you know about guitar?"

"You wouldn't think it to look at me now, but I used to be a garage band god. Not the video-game kind either like you whipper snappers. We practiced in a real garage. I used to wear an earring too. Don't you think a harmonica would be cheaper? I can get you a good Marine Band C harp for like ten bucks."

"Stocking stuffer, Dad."

Peter mopped up the last of the gravy on his plate with a bread roll. Indian summer lasted only two days. It had snowed the night before, and the weatherman predicted a bigger storm coming in over the weekend. A snow day to extend the holiday was a real possibility. Peter already was composing a list of films that he and Christy could watch. They'd recently discovered the joys of cheesy Hammer horror films. He was in charge of popcorn. She provided drinks. Most of the time they watched at her house because her parents had a sixty-inch screen, a kicker sound system, and a high tolerance for movies turned up loud.

The Sanders traveled for Thanksgiving, though, so he'd had an idea that if he could write essays, maybe he could write other stuff too. He'd spent the morning researching screenplay format. Dialogue didn't look that hard to make up. He had an idea for a science fiction film without special effects. Story rules, he thought. Explosions are just distractions so the audience doesn't notice you don't have a creative concept to start with.

"Cowboys versus the Lions for the afternoon game. Are you interested?" Dad looked longingly at the turkey, but must have decided a third helping would be pushing his luck.

"I've got a project. I'll pass. Great dinner, Dad. Thanks for cooking."

Dad smiled. "McDonald's was closed, or I'd just have sent you down there."

From his room, Peter heard the game playing. He lay on his bed, his hands laced behind his head, staring at the ceiling. What would he write? Was it really science fiction if the events actually happened? Wouldn't it be more of a documentary? He'd seen a great documentary on the Civil War, and another one of the Manhattan Project. Could he write about Wheeler, the Blue-suits and the gun as if it was a documentary? He could make it sound like a secret history: a story that used real history to tell a story that *could* have happened. Nothing historical could contradict it. H.G. Wells and Sir Arthur Conon Doyle were practically the same age, for example. He could write a story about the two of them meeting on a train from London to Edinburgh when Wells was fifteen and Doyle was twenty-two. That would be cool, a fifteen-year-old kid who would grow up to become a great science fiction writer hanging out with the guy who would become the great mystery writer. What if they got involved in a mystery on the train, a science fictional one? Peter could see the scene already: a steampunk Victorian railway car. Proper English ladies and gentleman heading north on business or to meet family, and the two, young men, one with a huge imagination, and the other with an understanding of deductive reasoning, seeing something happen, something small that no one else would notice, but the two of them did.

My mind is a weasel, thought Peter. I have this great, real story I can tell, and I'm thinking about Sherlock Holmes and *The Time Machine*. He laughed to himself. He could tell a story with Christy and Dante and himself in it. He'd change the names, of course. The ending would be different.

But he knew he'd be writing soon. He felt the same sort of pressure building within him he felt when he had a big essay assignment. He'd lay back as he was now, thinking about what he knew and what he wanted to say, and after a while, he'd have a first sentence. His computer was only two steps away. He'd push himself out of bed, put his hands on the keyboard, and go.

Wheeler went back to the world she belonged to days ago. Of all the images that stayed with him of the events, it was meeting her in the alley behind Goodman's Sporting Goods that seemed the clearest. She wore the long raincoat, kept her hands behind her back, and talked to him about the gun. "It's hazardous, son," she'd said. "It's dangerous beyond your comprehension."

Peter looked at the ceiling, glad in most ways that the adventure was behind him. Writing about it would be a way to keep it alive, though. He didn't want the experience to disappear like so much else did. He'd need to make notes, he realized. He could interview other people in town to get their perspectives on the events. Vice Principal Bovine, he thought, would be a very interesting interview. Peter hadn't heard what happened to Bovine at his house and why he missed school for the week.

He remembered the way the duffle bag felt when he first

picked it up, how the translucent bricks created the weight. When he held one up to the light, the tiny golden wires caught the sunlight. The brick had vibrated, he'd thought, when he first touched it. Wheeler said the bricks were what the story was about. All they needed were a little electricity, no more than a flashlight battery, and a switch to turn it on and off. A brick was "the heart of the gun." That would make a great title, he thought.

Not moving felt good. Dinner weighed him down pleasantly. Daydreaming about writing without writing felt good.

He studied his ceiling languidly, the way the tiles created a grid, the way the pattern in the tiles suggested shapes, like clouds. He looked at his ceiling vent.

The ceiling vent.

All thoughts of writing fled. He got up, closed and locked his bedroom door, then stood on the bed to open the ceiling vent. His fingers ran through dust and grit, but the brick was still there. He knew it when it buzzed for an instant against his skin.

Peter sat at his desk for a long time, the brick under his reading light, gold wires buried within, just as he remembered. Wheeler said that it took very little electricity. He found a package of double-A batteries in his desk, then straightened two paper clips to use as wires. When he held a clip to the battery's ends and touched the brick, the familiar hologram screen, filled with icons neatly in a row, flicked into existence. He broke the circuit. The screen disappeared, but he didn't move for the longest time.

In the myth, Pandora opened the box that released all the world's troubles. That was the story. Once the lid swung up, the troubles were out. There was no closing the lid again. Peter held the brick in his hand, thinking about Pandora kneeling beside the horrible box, her hand holding it open, and how she must have felt.

ABOUT THE AUTHOR

James Van Pelt teaches high school and college English in western Colorado. He has been publishing fiction since 1990, with numerous appearances in most of the major science fiction and fantasy magazines, including *Talebones, Realms of Fantasy, Alfred Hitchcock's Mystery Magazine, Analog, Asimov's, Weird Tales, SCIFI.COM*, and many anthologies, including several "year's best" collections. His first collection of stories, *Strangers and Beggars*, was released in 2002, and was recognized as a Best Book for Young Adults by the American Library Association. His second collection, *The Last of the O-Forms and Other Stories*, which includes the Nebula finalist title story, was released in August 2005 and was a finalist for the Colorado Blue Spruce Young Adult Book Award. His novel *Summer of the Apocalypse* was released November, 2006. His third collection, *The Radio Magician and Other Stories*, was released in 2009, and his fourth, *Flying in the Heart in the Lafayette Escadrille*, released in 2012. James blogs at http:// jimvanpelt.livejournal.com

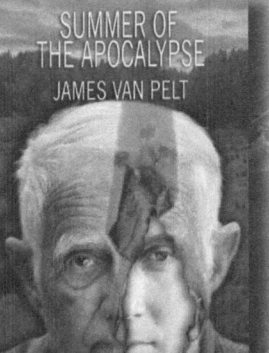
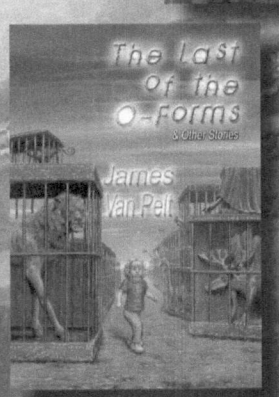

OTHER TITLES FROM FAIRWOOD PRESS

Cracking the Sky
by Brenda Cooper
trade paper: $17.99
ISBN: 978-1-933846-50-7

A Funeral for the Eyes of Fire
by Michael Bishop
trade paper: $17.99
ISBN: 978-1-933846-49-1

Blue Yonders, Grateful Pies
by Ken Scholes
trade paper: $17.99
ISBN: 978-1-933846-51-4

The Child Goddess
by Louise Marley
trade paper: $16.99
ISBN: 978-1-933846-52-1

The Court of Lies
by Mark Teppo
trade paper: $17.99
ISBN: 978-1-933846-44-6

The Best of Electric Velocipede
edited by John Klima
trade paper: $17.99
ISBN: 978-1-933846-47-7

Count Geiger's Blues
by Michael Bishop
trade paper: $17.99
ISBN: 978-1-933846-48-4

A Cup of Normal
by Devon Monk
trade paper: $16.99
ISBN: 978-0-9820730-9-4

www.fairwoodpress.com
21528 104th Street Court East;
Bonney Lake, WA   98391

www.ingramcontent.com/pod-product-compliance
Lightning Source LLC
Chambersburg PA
CBHW051255250626
47155CB00009B/3299